Memories
Are Forever

by
Anne Schraff

Perfection Learning® Corporation
Logan, Iowa 51546

Cover Illustration: Doug Knutson
Cover Design: Deborah Lea Bell

For information, contact:
Perfection Learning® Corporation
1000 North Second Avenue, P.O. Box 500
Logan, Iowa 51546-1099.
Tel: 1-800-831-4190 • Fax: 1-712-644-2392

Paperback ISBN 0-7891-4924-9
Cover Craft® ISBN 0-7807-8008-6
Printed in the U.S.A.

1 When the telephone rang, Bian rushed to answer it. Her father was sleeping, and she didn't want him to be disturbed. Mrs. Tran, Bian's mother, was in the kitchen making *cha gio*, a Vietnamese dish that contained chopped pork, mushrooms, and onions. As Bian reached for the phone, she thought how wonderful her mother's cooking always smelled. Bian had lived in California for five years now, since she was eleven, but she still loved Vietnamese food.

"Hi," Lucy Como, Bian's best friend, said. "I'm really stuck on the first two problems in geometry. I wondered if we could get together because I could sure use some help."

"Sure," Bian said. "My place or yours?"

"Um, better make it yours," Lucy said. "You know my grandfather. He doesn't like it when I have kids over."

Bian had known the answer to her question before she'd asked it. She had never been invited to Lucy's house, and she knew why. It wasn't that Lucy's grandfather didn't like *all* kids. It was just that he didn't like Vietnamese kids like her. He had been a soldier in the Vietnam War, and he had hated Vietnamese people ever since.

That war had ended when Bian's mother and father were very young. All Bian knew of it was what she had read in history books—and the horrible story Bian's father told of American pilots dropping napalm bombs on his village when he was only 12 years old. He still had scars on his arm from where the chemical had burned him. But Bian's father did not hate all Americans after the war. He had faith that people were basically good.

"Little one, the old ones cannot bury their ghosts," he had once explained to her in Vietnamese. Bian could still understand and speak her native language. "Lucy's grandfather cannot forgive, so he continues to fight. He is a prisoner of that terrible war."

Bian couldn't understand how someone could hate all people of a particular nationality just because some might be bad. She was glad that Buffalo Fraser's hatred hadn't rubbed off on Lucy.

"So I'll see you in a few minutes, okay?" Lucy said.

"Sure," Bian said. "Come on over."

A few minutes later, Lucy rode up on her brother's battered old bike. Lucy's father was often out of work, and they lived in one of the poorer sections of town. That was one of the reasons Lucy didn't have many friends. Like Bian, she was somewhat of an outsider looking for a place to fit in.

"I'm telling you," Lucy complained as she dropped her books on Bian's bed. "That Mrs. Phillips is the worst math teacher I've ever had. I've never been very good at math, but she's making geometry impossible for me to understand."

The girls worked for about 20 minutes. When Bian finished explaining bisecting angles, Lucy understood. She finished the rest of the problems by herself. When she was finished, she looked up. "You got any snacks around here? I'm starving."

Without thinking, Bian said, "My mother made *banh chung* this morning."

"What's that?" Lucy asked.

"Little rice cakes", Bian answered.

Lucy made a face. "Rice cakes? What's in them?"

"Ground pork and sweetened ginger root," Bian answered.

"That's not a snack," Lucy said. "I was thinking more on the lines of potato chips or cookies—you know, American food."

Bian blushed with embarrassment. She had forgotten how weird Lucy thought Vietnamese food was. Quickly she added, "I don't like them much either. How about some cookies?"

"Now you're talking," Lucy said.

She had put a package of chocolate chip cookies in her desk drawer after the last time Lucy had asked for a snack. She didn't know if her mother would approve, but sometimes it was hard being different from everyone else.

As she reached for two cookies, Lucy wrinkled her nose. "What's that weird smell coming from the kitchen?" she asked.

Again, Bian was embarrassed, but she rolled her eyes and said in an offhanded way, "Oh, my mother is making another of her famous dishes—some concoction of pork, mushrooms, and rice. I don't really like it. I only eat it so I don't hurt her feelings." Immediately she felt guilty for saying what she had said.

Lucy laughed. "Whew, that's a relief. I thought you were going to tell me she was cooking rat. That's what my grandfather says Vietnamese eat."

This time Bian could not hide the hurt she felt. "We would never do that, Lucy."

Lucy noticed her friend's reaction. "I know that, Bian," she said. "I was only teasing you. I don't believe half the things my grandfather says. He seems to get weirder every day."

"What do you mean?" Bian asked.

"Well, Mom says he was never right after he came home from the war. He spent a lot of time alone and had a lot of flashbacks."

"What are flashbacks?" Bian asked. This was a word she had never heard.

"They're like the worst kind of nightmares, only they can happen any time, not just at night. A lot of soldiers have them. A flashback can make a soldier think he's back in battle. Anyway, about a year ago Grandpa bought a

Harley-Davidson motorcycle, and now it's like he's back in the '60s. He wears his hair in a long, gray ponytail and rides around like he's a Hell's Angel or something. He's so weird that he's embarrassing. I mean, for crying out loud, he's in his fifties! I just wish he didn't live with us. I'm always afraid kids at school will find out he's my grandfather."

"Why does he live with you?" Bian asked. She remembered that extended families were very common in Vietnam. But here in California things were different.

"Mom says he's not stable enough to hold a job, so we let him move in with us when Grandma died. And lately he's been complaining of severe headaches, so she wants to be there to take care of him."

"Headaches?"

"Yeah, he says they're from the weed killers dropped on the jungles in South Vietnam to kill the trees. The Americans had to do that so they could see where the enemy was hiding."

"Doesn't that make him mad at the Americans?" Bian asked.

"Sort of, but it makes him more mad at

the Vietnamese. He says that if it weren't for them and their civil war, none of this would have happened."

Lucy got up to leave. "Well, I've got to go," she said. "Thanks a lot for the cookies—and for the help with geometry. You're a lifesaver."

Bian waved Lucy off and smiled to herself. They had only been friends for a year, but Bian really liked Lucy. She appreciated the fact that Lucy had offered her friendship when Bian had first moved to town. Lucy always told Bian that she was lonely too, and so they were a perfect match.

Bian's thoughts turned to Lucy's grandfather. Bian had seen him only once. He was a big man whose arms were covered with tattoos. Like Lucy said, he wore a long, gray ponytail and rode around on a big motorcycle. All in all, Bian thought he was a pretty threatening-looking guy. Lucy had told Bian that his real name was Barry Fraser, but nobody called him that. Everyone knew him as "Buffalo" Fraser. Her mother had never allowed Lucy to ask him about his nickname. All Lucy knew was that he had gotten the name in Vietnam.

Bian felt sorry that Buffalo Fraser hated Vietnamese people. She enjoyed talking to older people and would have liked to ask him why he was called Buffalo. But, of course, she was much too afraid to consider doing that.

A few minutes later as Bian was headed toward the kitchen to help her mother with dinner, Lucy called again. "You're never going to believe what just happened," she said. "I walked in the house and the phone was ringing. It was Clay Monroe. He wants me to go to the dance with him this weekend!"

"Clay Monroe?" Bian asked. Clay was a very popular senior. Bian was surprised that he would ask a shy sophomore like Lucy to the dance. "No offense, Lucy, but how did you manage that?"

"My brother got him to ask me. Mark owed me for not telling Mom and Dad that he didn't get home until 3:30 a.m. last Saturday."

"He's taking you out as a favor to your brother?" Bian asked.

"I know what you're thinking, Bian. It's

not the ideal way to get a date. But, hey, if I can impress Clay enough, he might ask me out again. You know I've always had a crush on him. Do you think you might go to the dance?"

"No one has asked me," Bian admitted. There were very few Asian boys at Drake High School. In fact, the only Vietnamese boy she knew was a genius who was more into computers than girls. Bian knew Thien Banh would never ask her to the dance.

There was a pause on the other end as if Lucy were thinking. Finally she said, "Hey, I know! Clay's best friend is Ken Peters. He and Mara Goldblum just broke up. Maybe Clay can get Ken to take you, Bian—then the four of us could go together."

"I don't know, Lucy," said Bian. She had never been to a dance at school, and she wasn't sure she knew how to act.

"Oh, come on, Bian," Lucy said. "It would be fun. If I can get up the nerve, I'll ask Clay at lunch tomorrow. We have the same lunch shift." Before Bian could protest further, Lucy hung up the phone.

As Bian put the receiver down, she

found that she was actually hoping Lucy would talk to Clay. She had seen Ken Peters a few times at school. He was a nice-looking boy who was well-liked by the other students. If Bian could go to the dance with him, maybe she could make a few more friends. Even though she was reluctant to admit it to Lucy or her parents, Bian would have preferred more of a social life than she had. Yet the more she thought about it, the more she realized how slim her chances were of getting a date with Ken. Bian knew how shy her friend was. Unless Lucy had changed, Bian doubted that she would be brave enough to actually approach Clay.

Bian went to the kitchen and set the table for three, knowing her father would join them to eat but would then hurry off to his job. Mr. Tran was the night janitor at a downtown hotel. Even though he had been a teacher in Vietnam, mastering a new language had been hard for him when he came to the United States. Since he still spoke very broken English, he was forced to take a job that did not require a lot of communication skills.

"You are fortunate to have a friend like Lucy," Mrs. Tran said at supper. Like Bian's father, Mrs. Tran had taken English at night school. But she had picked up the language very readily and now spoke it better than some Americans Bian knew. She used her command of the English language to communicate with her customers. Mrs. Tran was an excellent seamstress and did sewing for some of the ladies in the neighborhood. "She's a very nice girl. Are you making other friends at school too?"

"A few," Bian replied. "Lucy is my best friend, but I eat lunch with Trish and Bethany too."

"The students are nice at your school, eh?" Mr. Tran asked in Vietnamese.

"Most of them," Bian answered. She didn't mention the ones who said bad things to teachers or got into fights. There was no point in worrying her parents.

"Good, good," Mr. Tran managed to reply in English.

"Do you see Thien very often?" Mrs. Tran asked. Bian noticed that her mother had switched to Vietnamese so her father could understand.

"Not very often," Bian answered, also in Vietnamese. "He spends most of his free time in the computer lab. He's not really very sociable."

"Sociable is not so important," Mrs. Tran said. "He is a nice Vietnamese boy from a good family."

Bian's parents had known the Banh family in Vietnam. After moving to the U.S., Mr. and Mrs. Banh started a small restaurant in the suburbs. The two families often got together on weekends. Although they had never said it, Bian knew that her parents' wish was that she and Thien should marry someday.

"Maybe you should get interested in computers too, eh?" Mr. Tran teased.

Bian shrugged. "Maybe," she said. "But I'd like to get to know more American students too."

"American students are fine for casual friends," said Mrs. Tran. "But a Vietnamese boy is better for a good friend."

Bian thought about Ken Peters. How would her parents react if he asked her to the dance, she wondered.

In fifth period class the next day, Lucy had news for Bian.

"Guess what?" she cried. "I actually talked to Clay at lunch today, and he said he'd ask Ken about taking you to the dance. He seemed to like the idea of the four of us double-dating."

Bian looked at her beaming friend in amazement. Lucy had actually gone through with it! One date with a popular senior, and her shy friend was becoming an extrovert.

"You're going to say yes if he asks, aren't you?" Lucy asked.

"I guess so," Bian said. She could already feel her stomach churning with nervousness.

"What do you mean, you guess so?" Lucy demanded. "This is your chance—no, this is *our* chance to finally be noticed at this school. Don't you want to be more popular?"

Bian didn't know if she wanted to be popular or not. She simply wanted a few more friends, a little variety in her social life. Again, all she could say was, "I guess so."

After school that day Ken Peters approached Bian at her locker.

"Uh . . . Bian?" he asked uncertainly. Bian nodded, too nervous to speak.

"I was wondering . . . do you want to go to the dance with me Saturday?"

Bian lowered her eyes. "I—I think that would be nice," she stammered. "Thank you for asking."

"Okay, then, good," Ken said. "Pick you up at 7:30." He smiled at her before turning away. But Bian noticed that it was a lame smile, almost as if he were forcing it.

Still, Bian was excited as she biked home. Her first dance—and with a popular senior! Even if he never asked her out again, at least she would get to go to the dance, maybe meet new people, make a few new friends. She even had a new dress to wear. Her mother had been working on a beautiful black silk dress for the daughter of a woman down the street. The girl was away at college and needed a dress for a sorority function. Last week the woman had called and said that her daughter had to withdraw from college for health reasons and no longer needed the dress. She paid Mrs. Tran for her time and told her to sell the dress if she wanted to. Luckily, it was just Bian's size, so Bian's mother had decided to finish it for her. Now all Bian had to do was talk her parents into letting her go.

As Bian headed down the street, she noticed some commotion in the dead-end alley behind Swan's Ice Cream Parlor. Riding by slowly, she could hear loud, angry voices and laughter—the kind of laughter that makes a person afraid. Glancing up the alley, Bian saw Lucy's grandfather on his motorcycle trying to leave. A white pickup truck was blocking his way. Bian recognized two boys from Drake High in the cab of the truck— Tom D'Angelo and Gavin Hicks. Quietly, Bian pulled her bike behind some bushes and watched.

"Get out of my way, you little scumbags," Buffalo Fraser snarled, but the truck didn't move. He had a handkerchief tied around his head and was wearing a leather vest and pants. A song from the '60s was blaring from his bike radio.

"Hey, Grandpa," Tom shot back.

"Listening to your hippie music again?"

As Buffalo gunned his motor, Bian could see the numerous tattoos on his arms. "If you know what's good for you," he warned, "you'll move that rust bucket—now!"

"Oh, he's scary," Gavin laughed. "You scared, Tom?"

"Yeah, I'm afraid he'll hit us with his cane!" Tom said. Both boys laughed.

Bian noticed that Buffalo was slowly backing up his motorcycle. Soon he was next to the ramp of the loading dock behind the ice cream parlor.

"Where you going, Grandpa?" Gavin yelled. "There's no way out over there."

Suddenly, revving his engine hard, Buffalo flew up the ramp, sped to the end of the dock, and sailed over the pickup truck. He hit the alley hard, scattering dirt and gravel everywhere. Then he roared past Bian's hiding place and out of the alley. Bian could see him laughing as he raced by.

At first Tom and Gavin sat in stunned silence. Then Tom screamed, "Wait 'til next time, Grandpa! You're a dead man!"

But Buffalo Fraser was already down the street and around the next corner, well out of earshot.

2 The pickup truck tore through the alley, cut down the street, and roared away. Bian was sure neither Lucy's grandfather nor the boys from school had seen her as they left the alley.

She stood for a moment, catching her breath. The ugly scene she had just witnessed made her nauseous. She knew Tom and Gavin from school and did not like them. She had often heard them in the lunchroom making racial slurs about some of the students. But both boys were excellent basketball players, so they were rarely reprimanded for it. Gavin especially was a powerful center who had been high-scorer in the games several times this year. Thank goodness they hadn't seen her, Bian thought. So far she had avoided their negative attentions, and she wanted to keep it that way.

That evening Bian was very quiet as she helped her mother with supper. During the meal, she picked at her food.

"Are you all right, daughter?" Mrs. Tran asked.

When Bian looked up, she noticed that both parents were staring at her with concern. Bian wanted to tell them what she had seen in the alley. But she was afraid that if they knew that some of the American students were like Tom and Gavin, they would not let her go to the dance with Ken.

She managed to smile. "I'm fine," she said. "I was just thinking about the beautiful dress you are making me. It's a shame I have nowhere to wear it. I would love to show it to my friends at school, but of course, it's for a special occasion, like a dance."

Mrs. Tran beamed. Although she would never brag, she was proud of her skills and pleased that her daughter liked her work as well. "Are there no dances at your school?" she asked.

"Well, there's one Saturday night . . .," Bian began.

"Are you going?" her mother asked.

"Actually, I have been asked," Bian said.

Mrs. Tran raised her eyebrows. Then she turned and translated their conversation to her husband, who had been reading a Vietnamese newspaper.

Mr. Tran immediately put down his paper.

"Who asked you?" he asked. "Thien?"

Bian shook her head. "No, Thien does not like dances. He only likes computers. A very nice boy named Ken Peters asked me."

Mr. Tran narrowed his eyes. "An American?"

"Yes, but he's very nice," Bian repeated. "And we would be going with Lucy and her date."

"I'm sure he's very nice," said Mr. Tran. "And Lucy is also very nice. But in Vietnam, respectable girls don't go out with boys without an adult chaperone."

Bian was afraid her father would react that way. She turned to her mother for help. "Please, Mother," she said in English. "It's my chance to wear my beautiful dress."

Mrs. Tran looked sympathetic. Then she said softly to her husband in Vietnamese, "We are no longer in Vietnam, my husband. We left much behind in our old country. Just as we could not bring all of our possessions, we also could not bring all of our customs. It would be a shame if Bian should not have the chance to wear the dress."

Mr. Tran sighed and then smiled. "Very well," he said. "I can see that I am out-numbered here. In Vietnam, I would not allow myself to be outnumbered. But in America, majority rules, eh?" As quickly as it had come, his smile faded. "But just this once with this boy. Two dates with the same boy are not necessary. You are too young for such a relationship."

Bian could accept that. She had her doubts that Ken would ask her out again anyway.

When Lucy called that night, Bian told her the good news.

"Great!" Lucy said. "I can hardly wait."

"Me, too," Bian said. Then she lowered her voice so her parents wouldn't hear. "But I am so nervous. I don't know Ken at all."

"I don't know Clay very well, either," Lucy replied. "So we can lean on each other."

Suddenly Bian heard a loud slamming noise in the background. "What was that?" she asked.

Lucy groaned. "That's Grandpa coming in," she said. "He's in a really bad mood. He's been grumbling all evening. Something about some punk kids harassing him today. Oh, man, I hope it wasn't someone from school. I'll just die if anyone finds out he's my grandfather."

Bian decided it was not a good idea to tell Lucy about the incident in the alley. It would only upset her more.

"I'd better go," Lucy said. "See you tomorrow."

Saturday morning Bian and Lucy helped decorate the gym for the dance. The theme was "A Tropical Paradise." When they were finished, the gym was transformed into an exotic island, complete with palm trees, coconuts, and brightly colored birds.

Lucy and Bian stood back and surveyed their work. "This looks great," Lucy said. "It's so romantic!"

Bian agreed.

"Bian, I am so excited," Lucy said. "If tonight goes really well, maybe Clay will want to keep dating."

"I hope so, Lucy," Bian said. But secretly

she hated to see her friend set her hopes on the date with Clay. Since he was only taking Lucy out as a favor to her brother, Bian was afraid that any relationship between the two might be over before it had begun.

But despite her concerns for Lucy, Bian was excited about the dance as well. She hurried home from the gym to try on her dress one more time so her mother could do some final alterations.

When the dress was finished, Bian twirled before the full-length mirror on the bathroom door. Her mother had done a wonderful job. The dress looked exactly like the lovely party dresses at the mall. No one would guess it was homemade.

At 7:30, Ken rang the doorbell. Bian answered the door.

"Are you ready?" Ken asked. He made no effort to come inside.

"Yes, but first let me introduce you to my parents," Bian said.

Ken stepped inside, but Bian could tell he was uncomfortable. When Bian introduced Ken to her parents, he mumbled "Hi," then glanced sideways at Bian as if to say, "Can we go yet?"

Lucy and Clay were waiting for them in Clay's car. Bian noticed that Lucy was sitting right next to Clay, smiling up at him.

As they approached the car, Ken didn't bother to open the door for Bian. She climbed into the back seat and glanced at her house. Just as she expected, her parents were watching from the front window. Her father had a look of disapproval on his face.

"Hi, Bian," Lucy said gaily. She was carrying a beautiful pink nosegay that matched her pink satin dress.

"Hi," Bian said. She was already feeling disheartened about the evening. Ken hadn't brought her flowers, nor had he wanted to meet her parents. He obviously didn't want to be with her. Unlike Lucy, Bian hadn't expected the evening to be magical, but she had at least hoped to have a good time. Now that seemed unlikely.

Bian noticed that no one had said a word about her beautiful dress. She had at least expected a compliment from

Lucy, her best friend. Maybe Lucy was just too wrapped up in Clay to notice. But another fear was creeping into Bian's mind. Maybe her dress wasn't as beautiful as she thought. Maybe it was obviously homemade, and everyone at the dance would laugh at her.

All her life Bian had believed that her mother was a magical seamstress who made wonderful clothing. But perhaps she had been seeing the clothing through her love and admiration for her mother. It was like looking through the spectrum of a rainbow and seeing radiant colors in objects that were ordinarily dull and plain. Bian feared that she would stick out among the other girls like a weed in a flower bed.

The ride to the gym was almost unbearable. Ken didn't say a word. The silence between them was like a wall. Lucy, on the other hand, wasn't silent for a minute. She chattered incessantly and laughed at everything Clay said. She's trying too hard, Bian thought. Lucy put her arm around Clay's shoulders, while Clay nodded politely to her comments. She seemed oblivious to Clay's lack of interest.

A band was playing loudly as the four entered the gym. Bian looked around. The decorations hung earlier looked even more exotic with the aqua and pink lighting the industrial arts class had provided. Lucy had been right—it was romantic, or might have been had Bian been with someone other than Ken.

The gym was packed with students. Some were out on the dance floor gyrating to the music. Others were sitting at tables or standing around in groups, drinking punch and laughing. Looking at the beautiful dresses that surrounded her, Bian was even more self-conscious about her own. Every time she heard a giggle, she turned to see if someone were laughing at her.

The four sat at a table next to the dance floor. Almost immediately, Ken gravitated toward a group of his friends, leaving Bian with Lucy and Clay. But not for long. As soon as Clay had gotten the girls a glass of punch, Bian watched as Lucy pulled him onto the dance floor. The band was playing a slow song, and Lucy evidently saw it as her opportunity to get close—very close—to Clay. Poor Clay, Bian noticed. He looked as if he were being smothered.

"Bian," a familiar voice called. "Where did you get that dress?"

Bian turned sharply as if she had been struck. She was relieved to see that it was her friend Trish, whom she sometimes ate lunch with. Trish was with Nehru Cheddie. They had been dating for two years.

"Um, I got it at Lofton's," Bian lied. Lofton's was an exclusive teen store at the mall.

"It's fabulous!" Trish raved. "I love it."

"You do?" Bian looked closely at Trish to see if she were serious. She could detect no hint of mockery in her friend's face.

Just then Bethany walked by with her date. They were heading toward the refreshment table.

"Beth," Trish called. "Look at Bian's dress. Is it awesome or what? She got it at Lofton's."

"Wow, that is gorgeous, Bian," Bethany

said admiringly. "I wish I could afford that store. My mom made me buy mine at Penney's."

"Your dresses are very pretty too," Bian said. Instantly she felt ashamed for not giving her mother credit for the dress.

"Who's your date?" Trish asked, looking around.

"Um, Ken Peters," Bian said. "He'll be right back."

Nehru was nudging Trish to dance. "Well, have fun, Bian," Trish called over her shoulder as Nehru led her to the dance floor. Bethany and her date moved on to the refreshment table.

The rest of the evening couldn't have been more depressing for Bian. Ken stopped by a couple of times and even danced with her once, but he kept glancing at his watch as if he wished the evening were over. Lucy was so intent on impressing Clay that Bian saw almost nothing of her. To add to that, Bian kept reproaching herself for lying about the dress her mother had made her. All around her people were laughing and dancing. It seemed that everyone was having a good time except Bian.

About 10:00, someone approached Bian's table. She looked over to see Tom D'Angelo sitting down next to her!

"Hey, babe," he said. "What are you doing sitting here all by yourself?"

"I—I'm waiting for my friends," Bian stammered. Why was Tom at her table? Had he seen her in the alley the other day? Was he here to make trouble?

"Let me get you some punch," he offered. "You don't look too happy."

"I'm fine, thank you," Bian said, still confused. Before she could say any more, Tom disappeared with her cup. A minute later he was back.

"Here you go. This'll make you feel better." He handed her the cup filled to the brim with punch.

Bian really didn't want any more to drink. She had been sipping punch since she sat down simply to fill the time. But she didn't want to risk offending someone like Tom. She took the cup and raised it to her lips. But before she could take a sip, someone yelled, "Don't drink that!"

3 Bian jumped, nearly dropping her cup. Standing above Tom was Clay Monroe. He looked angry.

"I saw what you did, man," Clay said.

"Mind your own business," Tom snarled back.

Bian looked at Clay questioningly. "He spiked your drink," Clay explained. "I saw him."

Clay had been at the refreshment table waiting for Lucy, who was in the restroom "powdering her nose." He had watched as Tom had taken a small flask out of his pocket and poured some of the contents into Bian's cup.

"Get lost, D'Angelo," Clay said. "Or I'll turn you in."

Tom cursed at Clay under his breath. Then he stomped off.

Clay sat down. "That jerk likes to bring booze and spike kids' drinks," he said. "I've seen him do it before."

"Thank you," Bian said, her voice barely above a whisper. Clay had done her a great favor. Bian had never had alcohol before. She might have drunk the spiked punch and gotten sick—or worse yet, made a complete fool of herself and disgraced her parents.

"Where's Ken?" Clay asked.

Bian was embarrassed to admit that she didn't know. She shrugged her shoulders slightly and looked down at the table.

Clay noticed her embarrassment. "Would you like me to go find him?" he asked softly.

Now Bian was close to tears. The whole evening had been a disaster, from Ken ignoring her to Tom trying to take advantage of her. Without looking up, Bian shook her head.

Clay reached over and lifted her chin with his finger. Bian noticed that his hand smelled slightly of cologne. She liked the smell. "Hey, I'm sorry about the way Ken's treating you," he said. "Guess D'Angelo isn't the only jerk here tonight, huh?"

Just then Lucy came back to the table. Clay quickly removed his hand.

"Did I miss anything?" Lucy asked.

"No," said Clay nonchalantly. "Just Tom D'Angelo trying to spike Bian's punch."

"Oh, Bian, are you all right?" Lucy

asked. "You look like you're about to cry."

But before Bian could answer, the band started playing a song with a pulsating rhythm, and Lucy pulled Clay back onto the dance floor. Again, Bian was amazed at her friend's behavior. Bian wondered if she would be acting the same way if she were trying to impress Ken.

Ken came back to the table about ten minutes later, just as the band was finishing up for the evening with a slow song.

"Do you want to dance?" he asked.

Bian knew he felt obligated to ask her. "No, thank you," she answered. She didn't want to give him the satisfaction of feeling as if he had "fulfilled his duty."

When the song ended, Lucy and Clay returned. "You two ready to go?" Clay asked Ken. It was 10:30.

"Yeah," Ken answered. "Um . . . I should be home by 11:00."

Clay glanced at Ken sideways. It was obvious he knew Ken was lying.

"Don't go home, Ken," Lucy begged. "Let's all go to Kelsey's." Kelsey's was a nice restaurant in town that sold steaks and seafood as well as pizza.

"No, I've got to get up early," Ken said. "My dad and I are going hunting. But Bian can go if she wants."

Bian glanced at Lucy, who was looking at Bian as if to say, "Please say no. I want to be alone with Clay." Now that they wouldn't be there as two couples, Lucy didn't want Bian along.

Bian opened her mouth to turn down the offer just as Clay spoke up. "Good idea," he said. Then he noticed that Lucy was glaring at him. "Um . . . I mean, how often does a guy get a chance to be seen with not one, but *two* beautiful girls?"

Lucy looked appeased, and Ken seemed relieved that his "date" was being taken care of. "So it's settled then," Ken said. "You can drop me off at home."

A few minutes later, they pulled into Ken's driveway. As Ken got out of the car, he glanced at Bian and said, "Thanks. I had a good time." Then the door closed, and Bian was left sitting in the back seat alone.

Bian doubted that he'd had a "good time." Or if he had, she knew it was with his friends, not with her.

At Kelsey's, Bian and Lucy went to the restroom together. Bian ran a quick comb through her long, dark hair, touched up her lipstick, and was finished. Lucy, on the other hand, took out an arsenal of makeup, combs, and hair spray. "You go ahead," she said. "Tell Clay I'll be right out."

It was obvious Lucy was going to be there awhile, so Bian went back to the table.

As Bian approached the table, she noticed that Clay seemed to be deep in thought. He was staring hard into his soft drink as he stirred it with a straw.

"Lucy will be right out," Bian said, sitting down. "What are you reading in there, your fortune?" she added jokingly.

"Guess I am, sort of," Clay said, smiling. "I was just thinking about tonight—and about the future."

"About your future with Lucy?" Bian asked. Maybe she could get a good word in for her friend. "She really likes you."

Clay shrugged noncommittally. "Yeah, I know," he said.

"She's a very nice girl," Bian added.

"And very pretty."

"Yeah, she's real nice," said Clay. "But I really only took her out as a favor to her brother. I realize now that was wrong."

Bian hesitated a minute, then said quietly, "Like Ken taking me out as a favor to you?"

Clay looked at her and smiled. "Guess I had that coming, didn't I?" Then his tone became more serious. "Hey, I'm really sorry about tonight."

"It's all right," Bian answered.

"No, it's not all right," Clay said. "Here you were all dressed up and ready to have a good time, and look what happened. By the way, did I tell you what an awesome dress that is?"

Bian blushed and shook her head.

"Well, it is," Clay said. "And you look great in it. I mean it."

Bian started to say, "I got it at Lofton's," but then decided that this time she would not betray her mother. She looked directly at Clay and said, "My mother made it."

Clay was obviously impressed. "You're kidding?" he said. "Man, you must have one talented mother."

"I do," Bian answered proudly. It felt good to be talking about her mother like that. But at the same time, she didn't know how to take such a personal compliment about her dress from her best friend's date.

"You know, I was born in Korea," Clay said. "My dad was in the Army. We lived there 'til I was ten. I remember it pretty well."

"That's interesting," said Bian. "I'm from Vietnam."

"Is that close to Korea?" Clay asked.

"No, not really," Bian smiled. "But I guess you could say it's in the general area. Did you like Korea?"

"Yeah, I really did, especially the people. Sometimes when my parents went out, a Korean girl would come watch me. Her name was Kim." He laughed softly as if recalling a sweet memory. "I had the biggest crush on her. She had the most beautiful eyes I'd ever seen." He paused, then lowered his voice and said, "Eyes like yours, Bian."

"Thank you," Bian said, squirming a little. Again, she was uncomfortable, so she decided to change the subject. "I wonder where Lucy is," she said, looking around. "Oh, here she comes now."

Lucy definitely looked "freshened up" when she came back to the table. Her makeup and hair were perfect. But Bian noticed that her friend was wearing more mascara than she'd ever seen her wear before. Bian thought it made her look rather unnatural, but she didn't say anything.

"Clay, I hope you had as much fun tonight as I did," Lucy said when she sat down.

"I don't know," Clay said. "How much fun did you have?"

Bian knew he was trying to avoid the subject by making a joke. But Lucy looked hurt, and Bian felt sorry for her.

Suddenly Bian wished she hadn't come. Maybe if she weren't there, Clay would pay more attention to Lucy.

While they waited for their order, Lucy chattered away at Clay. Clay, however, said very little, so Bian did her best to keep the conversation going. It was not easy, though, because every time her eyes met Clay's, she detected something in them that made her stumble over her words.

Finally, the evening ended, and Clay and Lucy took her home. As she got out of the car, she mumbled a thank-you to Clay and told Lucy she would call her tomorrow. Then she headed toward the house, both sad and confused.

"Chao anh," Mrs. Tran greeted her daughter in Vietnamese. "Was the dance all you hoped it would be?"

Before she could answer, her father asked, "How did the American boy treat you?"

She knew if she told her parents the truth, they would never let her date another American boy. For some reason, the image of Clay popped into her head.

"It was fine," she said, forcing a smile. "And the American boy was a perfect gentleman. In fact, he loved my dress." She neglected to say *which* American boy she was referring to.

"Good, good," her father said in English, and her mother looked pleased.

That night Bian couldn't sleep. Every

time she closed her eyes, she saw Clay's face across the table from her. What did she detect in his eyes? Or was she just imagining that she detected something?

* * *

On Sunday, Bian's family went to Thien's house for dinner. Of course, Bian found Thien at the computer. His computer skills were so widely known at school that the kids had nicknamed him Mouse.

"I did not see you at the dance last night, Thien," Bian said.

"I am too busy for such nonsense," Thien said. "I suppose you went?"

Bian nodded.

"And did you have a good time?" Thien wanted to know.

"Actually, no," Bian said. "My date ignored me, and my girlfriend's date paid too much attention to me."

Thien nodded his head knowingly. "I am not surprised. American adolescents become involved in relationships too early. They don't know how to handle them."

"All I know is I feel really guilty about what happened," Bian said. "I mean, Lucy Como is my best friend—and she's just crazy about this guy."

"Who is it?" Thien asked.

"Clay Monroe. He's a senior," Bian answered.

Thien laughed grimly, his fingers moving swiftly to guide the arrow across his computer screen. "Oh, yes, I know him. He's in my computer graphics class. I was there when Lucy's brother approached Clay about taking her to the dance. He practically had to beg him. If Lucy thinks Clay is her boyfriend, she is dreaming."

"What should I do, Thien?" Bian asked.

"Simple. Stay away from boys. Wait until after college to have a relationship. That's what I am going to do. School first, relationships second." He displayed a radiant jumble of symbols on his monitor. "I am building my home page. What do you think of it?"

"It's very nice," Bian said. She decided Thien was right. She should forget Clay. When his face came to her mind, she should dismiss it like the memory of a bad dream.

As Bian's father pulled the car into the driveway that evening, Lucy rode up on her bike.

"Oh, Bian," Lucy cried. "I need to talk to you. Let's go to Swan's so we can talk in private."

"Sure," Bian said. But as she got on her bike, she had a sinking feeling in her stomach. Had Lucy seen what had passed between Clay and Bian?

As the girls headed for the ice cream parlor, they passed the alley where Buffalo Fraser had been confronted by Gavin and Tom. Bian glanced up the alley. She was glad to see that it was deserted now.

The girls ordered sundaes and sat down in the far corner of the ice cream parlor. For a few minutes, Lucy didn't say anything. She just sat and stabbed at her sundae like she was mad at it. The sinking feeling in Bian's stomach got worse. Finally Lucy burst out, "Oh, Bian, what am I doing wrong? Clay can't stand me!"

Bian didn't know what to say. She was relieved that Lucy wasn't angry at her.

But she also remembered Thien's words: "If Lucy thinks Clay is her boyfriend, she is dreaming." She had no idea how to comfort her friend without being dishonest. Finally she offered weakly, "I thought the two of you got along pretty well."

"Oh, come on, Bian," Lucy said. "He was as cold as ice to me all night. He didn't even kiss me goodnight!"

Bian reached out and patted Lucy's hand. "Perhaps you are trying too hard," she said softly, hoping she was not hurting her friend's feelings. But ironically, just the opposite happened.

"That's it, Bian!" Lucy cried.

"It is?"

"Yes! Well, no, not that I'm trying too hard—that I'm not trying hard *enough!*" Lucy cried. "Let's see . . . what should I do? I know! Our youth group at the church has a dance coming up in two weeks. I'm going to ask him to it."

"Are you sure you want to do that, Lucy?" Bian asked.

"Why not?" Lucy said. "I'll get a new dress, have my hair done—he won't be able to resist me!"

"Lucy," Bian said. "I've never seen you like this. It's like you are an entirely different person where Clay is concerned."

"I know, Bian," Lucy said. "But I just like him so much. And I want him to like me."

Bian took a deep breath. She had to try to stop this before Lucy got hurt even more. "Lucy," she began, "boys are funny, don't you think? I mean, they don't always want what they appear to want."

"What do you mean?" Lucy asked.

"Well, Clay asked you to the dance, but maybe he doesn't really want a steady girlfriend. My friend Thien says kids our age don't know how to handle relationships. Maybe Clay isn't ready for a relationship yet."

"Bian, that's crazy," Lucy said. "Everybody dates. That's why you go to high school. Or at least that's the only thing that makes high school fun."

Bian stirred her sundae and stared into the golden swirls. Without looking up, she said, "Lucy, I think Thien is right. He's very clever. Maybe we should just forget about boys."

Lucy was silent for so long that Bian glanced up. Her friend had a strange look on her face. It was a look Bian had never seen before, so she had no idea what to make of it. "Bian," Lucy asked, "did Clay tell you something Saturday night? Something I should know?"

4 Bian was trembling inside. She knew she should tell Lucy about what had happened, but she didn't want to hurt her feelings. So she just said, "Like what?"

"Oh, I don't know," Lucy said. "I thought maybe he found out about my weird grandfather or something."

Again, Bian was relieved. "Oh, no," she said. "He said nothing about your grandfather."

"Good," Lucy said. "Now, let's see. I've got some money saved, and my brother owes me twenty-five dollars. Maybe my mom will add to it and help me buy another dress . . ."

Bian headed home, leaving Lucy pondering how she could swing the cost of a new dress. As she rode up the driveway, she noticed her elderly neighbor, Mr. Lamansky, was out trimming his hedge.

"Hi, Mr. Lamansky," Bian called as she pulled her bike into the carport. "How are you?"

"Well, I'm still going," Mr. Lamansky laughed. "That's what counts when you're my age."

Mr. Lamansky had a son who had served as a surgeon in the Vietnam War. His son had developed such a fascination with the culture that after the war, he had gone back to Vietnam to live. He had opened a clinic to provide affordable health care for the Vietnamese people while the country recovered from the devastating effects of the war.

"What do you hear from your son?" Bian asked as she approached the hedge.

"Just got a letter this week," Mr. Lamansky said. "He's now head of surgery at one of the hospitals in Ho Chi Minh City."

"That's wonderful," Bian said. Bian was familiar with Ho Chi Minh City. The Trans had come from a village not far from there. "I have a friend whose grandfather fought in the war."

"Who's that?" Mr. Lamansky asked.

"He's called Buffalo. Buffalo Fraser," Bian said.

"Think I know the fellow you're talking about," Mr. Lamansky said. "Wears a ponytail? Rides a motorcycle?"

"That's him," Bian said.

"Sad story there," Mr. Lamansky said. "He's let the past get the best of him. My son saw the worst of the war too. Couldn't help it, being a surgeon and all, you know. But he moved on, made something of his life. Some people just can't do that. It's like they look for an excuse to be unhappy, like they're happier being unhappy. Does that make sense?"

Bian nodded. "How did he get that name—Buffalo? Do you know?"

"I heard once. Evidently the boys in his unit were dying off pretty fast. The ones that were left had this grim joke that they were like the buffalo, on the verge of extinction. Turns out he was the only one who survived—the last buffalo. When he left Vietnam, he took the name as a kind of tribute to the guys in his unit. I guess he still uses it all these years later because he can't forget that part of his life. Some memories are forever."

Bian considered what Mr. Lamansky had said. Then she told him, "I feel sorry for Mr. Fraser. He seems very lonely."

"I'm sure he is," Mr. Lamansky said. Then he smiled. "You've got a good heart, little lady. I hope it stays that way."

Bian entered the house, still worrying about Lucy. She resolved not to have anything to do with Clay Monroe, not just for Lucy's sake, but for her own as well. Thien was right. She should avoid relationships until she was older. Look what trying to get a boyfriend was doing to Lucy!

The next morning at school, Bian saw Clay leaning on her locker as she approached. She could feel her heart beating faster. "I must stick to my resolution," she told herself.

"Good morning," he said cheerfully.

"Good morning," Bian said. "Excuse me, I must get into my locker."

Clay moved out of the way. "Are you busy Friday night?" he asked, as Bian took her English book out.

Bian thought fast. "Yes," she said. "I am going to the basketball game with my friend Thien."

"That's too bad," Clay said, looking disappointed. "I was going to ask you to go with me."

Bian pretended to be digging in her

locker for a lost book so she wouldn't have to look at him. "Why don't you take Lucy?" she asked casually.

Clay shrugged. "I don't know," he said.

Lucy walked up as Bian closed her locker. "What are you guys talking about?" Lucy asked, frowning.

"The basketball game Friday night," Bian said. "We were discussing our chances for going to state." Bian surprised herself. She was getting good at this.

Lucy smiled broadly and looked up at Clay. "I'm free Friday night, Clay, if you need someone to go with."

Clay looked confused. "Um, yeah, okay," he mumbled. Quickly he turned and walked away.

"Yes!" Lucy cried. "Yes! He asked me to the game! Did you see that, Bian?"

Bian smiled. "I'm very happy for you," she said. And for myself, she thought. Now I just have to talk Thien into going to the game with me.

Bian tracked Thien down at lunch. "Please, Thien," she begged. "You have to go with me. Just this once."

"But I hate basketball," Thien complained. "Such a waste of time trying to get a silly ball into a wire basket just so it falls out again."

"But if you don't come, it will look like I have no boyfriend, and Clay will ask me out again. Please, Thien. I would do it for you."

"Oh, all right," Thien finally conceded. "But I will hate every minute of it."

"Oh, Thien, you are truly a kind person," Bian said.

"Don't get gushy," Thien said.

On Friday night, the gym was packed for the game. The Drake Dragons were now playing their crosstown rival, the Lincoln Lynx, for the district championship. Whichever team won would go to state. Center Gavin Hicks was the main reason the team had gotten so far in the conference. Tom D'Angelo put plenty of points on the scoreboard too. Bian usually went to the games to cheer for the Dragons, but she hated to see boys like Gavin and Tom get the glory. The more points the two racked up at the games, the more arrogant and cruel they seemed to become.

As Bian and Thien sat down, Bian noticed that some of the students had painted their faces half purple and half gold, the school's colors. Others had on masks made out of basketballs. Several boys at the top of the bleachers were shirtless. They had letters painted on their chests so that when they stood up, they formed the word "Dragons."

Bian thought it was very strange and thrilling in a way, but Thien shook his head in disgust.

"It is all so ridiculous," he said, hardly looking up from his computer supply catalog. He was planning on adding memory to his computer and was thumbing through the advertisements for the best deal. "Look at that," he said, pointing at the huge dragon mascot parading around the floor. "In Vietnam, the dragon is the most revered of all creatures. Here in America, he prances around a gymnasium while people with basketballs on their heads cheer." He shook his head. "Insane."

As Bian sat looking around, she saw

that Clay and Lucy had come in. She couldn't believe it when Lucy spotted her in the crowd and steered Clay toward them.

"Scoot down," Lucy said. "We'll sit by you."

Bian started to shake her head no, but Thien was already moving down. Before she knew it, Clay Monroe was sitting right next to her!

5 Clay looked her directly in the eyes. "Hi," he said. Bian was too flustered to answer.

For most of the first half, the two teams were neck and neck. Then Gavin and Tom each made a three-pointer, and the Dragons took the lead. The Lynx had several turnovers, and the Dragons, fired up now, piled points on the board.

But Bian saw little of the game. Every time Clay sat down after standing up to cheer, his thigh brushed hers. When he leaned across her to say something to Thien about the game, she could smell his cologne—the same cologne he had on the night of the dance. Once his hand even touched hers.

As halftime approached, Bian felt something at her elbow. When she turned, she was almost surprised to see Thien tugging at her sleeve. She had nearly forgotten he was there.

"Do you want to move during the half?" Thien whispered, nodding toward Clay.

Bian shook her head. She knew if they moved, Lucy would wonder why. Thien returned to his catalog.

At halftime the score was 47–41, with the Dragons in the lead. As the teams headed for the locker rooms, the pulsating bass beat of Queen's "We Will Rock You" filled the gym. The mascots for the two teams pretended to duke it out on the sidelines.

When Lucy and Clay got up to go to the refreshment stand, Bian got an idea.

"Thien, trade places with me," she said.

Thien looked at her knowingly and then shrugged. "Whatever," he said.

When Clay and Lucy returned, Bian did not look at Clay's face to see his reaction to the new seating arrangement. She was just grateful to escape the tension caused by sitting next to him.

The second half of the game had fewer surprises. It seemed the Lynx could do nothing right, and the Dragons could do nothing wrong. Gavin Hicks racked up a total of 32 points for the game and Tom D'Angelo scored 26. The final score was 73–54. The Dragons were on their way to state, and the Drake fans went into a frenzy. Hundreds of them mobbed the floor, carrying Gavin and Tom off on their shoulders.

"Oh, great," Thien remarked dryly. "That ought to feed their egos."

As they filed out of the gym, Bian saw Lucy clinging to Clay's arm.

"What do you want to do now?" she heard her ask.

"I've got to get home, Lucy," said Clay. "I'm sorry. But I've got a journalism project due soon. I should get started on it."

Lucy looked crushed. Just then her brother Mark came by with a group of kids. "Hey, we're going out for pizza," he said. "You two want to come?"

Clay said, "Sorry, I can't. I was just telling Lucy I've got to get home."

"Why don't you come with us, Luce?" Mark asked. "And you too." He nodded at Bian and Thien. "The more, the merrier!"

Lucy shrugged. "I guess I might as well. See you later, Clay?" Bian could hear the hope in her voice.

"Yeah, later," Clay said. "Hey, thanks for coming to the game with me."

Lucy, Bian, and Thien followed the group to the parking lot. There they got into their cars and drove to Rick's Pizza Palace. At the restaurant, they pushed several tables together and sat down to order.

While waiting for the pizza, Bian heard Lucy complain to her brother, "Clay treats me like I don't exist. He wouldn't even come out for pizza tonight."

"Well, he asked you to the game, didn't he?" Mark asked.

"Sort of. Actually I asked him," Lucy said.

Mark sighed. "Look, Luce," he said. "I did my part. I got him to take you to the dance. I can't get him to like you. Why don't you just give up on him? Face the fact that he only went out with you as a favor to me. You're obsessed with this guy—and it's getting embarrassing."

Again, Bian felt sorry for the rejection Lucy was feeling. But she felt sorry for Clay too. Clay had done a friend a favor by taking his sister to a dance. It wasn't his fault that Lucy was reading all kinds of things into that simple act of friendship.

Thien whispered in Bian's ear. "Do you see how ridiculous this is becoming? The stupidity of high school romance! Clay is not interested in Lucy. Lucy is acting like a betrayed wife. It's all crazy. It would be laughable if it did not cause so much pain for all involved."

"Oh, Thien," Bian said. "I wish I was as sure about all this as you are."

On the way home, Bian and Thien passed groups of happy Drake students out celebrating the victory. Traffic was very congested, and Thien had to drive slowly. It was then that Bian noticed the motorcycle in back of them. Buffalo Fraser was cruising the crowded street. Suddenly Buffalo roared past Thien's car, glaring at the two of them. "Get out of my way, you gooks!" he yelled. "Why don't you go back where you came from?"

"Well," Thien said, "you have a nice day too, sir."

"He is a very sad man," Bian explained. "I have seen him around town." She didn't mention that he was Lucy's grandfather because she had promised not to.

As Thien pulled into Bian's driveway, she said, "Thank you for taking me to the game."

Thien grinned. "Oh, it was nothing. I enjoy being bored out of my mind."

* * *

Sunday morning, the phone rang at Bian's house. Her father answered it. "It is for you," he said solemnly. "A young man." Bian noticed that his eyebrows had a disapproving arch to them as he returned to the program he was watching on television.

At the sound of Clay's voice, Bian's heart beat faster. "Bian? This is Clay. How are you doing?"

"I am fine," Bian answered.

"Say, I was just wondering," Clay went on. "I've got this big journalism project due soon. I have to write a series of articles about the different ethnic groups at our school. Anyway, there's an ethnic fair at City Park downtown today. There's going to be all kinds of food and music, and arts and crafts."

Clay paused.

"Yes?" Bian asked.

"Well, there's an exhibit on Vietnam. And I thought maybe you could go with me and help me understand the Vietnamese culture better."

"I don't know," said Bian. She glanced at her father, who appeared to be watching television. But Bian knew he was listening to her every word, hoping to make sense of what she was saying based on the few English words he knew.

"Come on, it'd be fun," Clay said.

Bian had read some of Clay's articles in the *Drake Drum Roll*, the school newspaper that was published once a month. Bian liked the way he wrote, and even before she knew him, she thought he was the best staff writer on the paper. But go to the ethnic fair with him? She had promised herself she would avoid him. Still, this was different than a date, she rationalized. Helping him understand the customs of her people for his article could increase tolerance of all ethnic groups at the school. The article might even reach students like Gavin and Tom.

"I'm not sure," she said. "I'll have to ask my parents."

"Okay," Clay said. "I'll hold on."

As Bian laid down the phone, her

mother came into the room and sat in her sewing chair. She was hemming a skirt for a customer.

Bian spoke in Vietnamese for her father's benefit. "A boy who writes for the school newspaper would like me to go to the ethnic fair with him. He wants me to help him understand the Vietnamese culture so he can write an article about it for the newspaper."

Without looking up from the television her father said, "This boy, he is American?"

"Yes," replied Bian with an even voice.

"The same boy who took you to the dance?"

"No, Father, a different one."

Mrs. Tran put down her sewing. "It would seem a very good thing for Bian to do," she said to her husband. "This boy must have much respect for her to ask her help in this important task."

"That is true," Mr. Tran said. "You may go, Bian," he said. "But you must be home by 5:00."

Returning to the phone, Bian told Clay, "Yes, I can go with you." She tried not to sound too excited.

"Great, I'll pick you up about 11:00. We'll eat lunch there."

Bian thought about Lucy as she put down the phone. What if she found out? Bian would feel awful. Still, it wasn't like it was a date. She was simply helping Clay out. But even if it were a date, did Lucy really have a right to be mad at her? Lucy's own brother had said that Clay had only gone out with her as a favor to him. It was not fair that Lucy had decided Clay was her boyfriend when Clay had never been part of the decision.

Bian spent the next hour doing her hair and trying to decide what to wear. She scolded herself for such foolish behavior, but still she searched her closet for just the right sweater to go with her new jeans. She kept telling herself that this was not a date. It was more like an educational assignment. She was assisting a reporter with an article about her own people. What could be more innocent than that?

But Bian had to admit to herself that she would not be this excited about an ordinary assignment. If she were going to the ethnic fair with her history class, she would not feel so giddy. She wouldn't be trying on her blue sweater, pulling it off, then trying on her yellow sweater, and also removing that until she finally settled on the red one.

Bian turned before the mirror, making sure the red sweater was the right choice. She decided it looked very becoming against her olive skin and dark hair. She arranged her hair one more time and then went into the living room to wait for Clay.

Unlike Ken, Clay was not reluctant about meeting her parents. He smiled politely and even sat down for a few minutes and told them about his life as a child in Korea. Bian translated for her father. She listened to Clay with admiration. Even though he was only seventeen, he had the charm and manners of a much older person. Bian could tell her parents were impressed by him.

"I think it is very interesting that you work on the school newspaper," Bian said as they headed toward the park in Clay's car. "I bet you get to meet a lot of fascinating people."

Clay smiled. "Fascinating *and* beautiful," he said, looking directly into her eyes. "By the way, you look great in that sweater. It makes your eyes look even darker than they are."

"Um, thank you," Bian said, searching in her mind for a way to change the subject. "My friend Thien is a fascinating person. Perhaps you could interview him."

"Mouse? He's fascinating, all right. I've never known anyone who knows computers better than he does. We were having problems with one of the computers in the lab the other day. Along comes Mouse and has it working in no time. I think his brain is a hard drive."

"What do you want to do after high school, Clay?" Bian asked.

"Write," Clay answered. "I'm going to major in journalism next year at college. That's why I'm on the newspaper now, for the experience. How about you? What do you want to do when you graduate?"

"I might be a math teacher," Bian said. "But I'm not sure. I think I would like teaching girls because girls are often afraid of mathematics. Or they're convinced it's too hard. I think I could make it easier for them."

Clay pulled his car into the parking lot across from City Park, and the two started walking toward the ethnic fair. After a few steps, Clay reached over and took Bian's hand. Quickly Bian pulled her hand away, but her fingers felt as if they tingled with electricity.

"Clay, this is not a date," Bian reminded him.

Clay stopped. "Look, Bian," he said, taking her hand again. "There's no sense lying to you. I wanted you to come and help me understand the exhibits and all that. But my real reason for asking you here today was because I like you—a lot. Don't you feel anything for me at all?" He looked directly into her eyes as he spoke.

Bian was flustered. She said nothing at first. But no matter how hard she fought it, she knew she liked Clay too. Her fingers were still tingling as he held her hand, and her heart was pounding.

Bian started to speak but then caught her breath sharply as she glanced over

Clay's shoulder. Riding toward them on their bikes were Lucy and Bethany—and they were looking right at them!

6 "Look, she would have found out sooner or later anyway," Clay was saying as they ate *nuoc mam*. They were sitting at a little table under a brightly colored awning. Clay had insisted on eating authentic Vietnamese food even though hamburgers and hot dogs were available at various stands in the park. Bian normally loved the rice covered with a rich, brown fish sauce, but today she could barely taste it. She was feeling too bad for Lucy.

"But what a terrible way to find out!" Bian said, shaking her head sadly. Lucy and Bethany had ridden by without a word. Now Bian couldn't get the look of hurt and anger on her friend's face out of her mind.

"Bian, I was never dating Lucy," Clay explained. "I simply did her brother a favor. I can't help it if she still has a crush on me. Believe me, I didn't encourage her."

"I know that," Bian said. "But Lucy doesn't."

"Think of it this way, Bian," Clay said. "If you saw Ken Peters here today with another girl, would it bother you?"

"No, he does not like me. He only took me to the dance as a favor to you," Bian answered.

"Exactly. You figured that out right away and went on with your life. Lucy hasn't figured it out yet. Or at least if she has, she won't admit it. But it's high time she did. I don't mean to be cruel, but it's better this way. In the end, she'll be hurt less."

Bian knew he was probably right. She had been hurt the night of the dance when Ken ignored her. But it was better than if he had acted like he liked her and then she had found out the truth later.

Clay put down his fork. "I couldn't eat another bite," he said. "That was delicious." He offered her his hand. "Come on. Let's do what we came here to do. Show me around."

Despite her sadness for Lucy, Bian felt a thrill of anticipation as she took Clay's hand. She made up her mind to enjoy her day with him. She could try to smooth things over with Lucy later.

"So," said Clay as they approached a booth of Vietnamese gift items. "Why is so much stuff red?"

An older Vietnamese woman in the booth smiled at them. She was dressed in the traditional *ao dai*, a long tunic with slits on either side and full trousers.

"Red is a happy, lucky color," Bian explained. She glanced down at her sweater. Perhaps that's why I chose to wear this, she thought.

"And I see lots of bird shapes," Clay said, picking up a necklace with a bird-shaped pendant.

"The *chim-phuong-hoang* is a mythical bird. It is also a sign of good luck," Bian said.

"Do you like this?" Clay asked, holding up the necklace.

"Very much," Bian answered. "It reminds me of a necklace my grandmother used to wear."

"Is your grandmother lucky?" Clay teased.

Bian felt a pang of sadness. Her grandmother had died almost five years ago. But, of course, Clay didn't know that. And today was not the day to bring up sad things. Instead, Bian smiled and said,

"She always said she was very lucky to have a granddaughter like me."

Clay smiled too. "She sounds like a very smart lady," he said. "I think she would want you to have this." Before Bian could protest, Clay had paid for the necklace. "Turn around," he said. "I'll hook it for you."

Bian turned around and lifted her long hair out of the way. Again, her skin tingled as Clay brushed the back of her neck with his fingers. "There," he said. "Let me see how it looks on you." He turned her around gently. "Perfect!"

"Thank you," she said softly. "You are very generous." Hand in hand, they headed to the next exhibit, where they watched a Vietnamese puppet show. "What is the story about?" Clay asked as they sat down in folding chairs in front of the stage.

"It is the story of how the Vietnamese were descendants of a dragon-lord and a fairy princess," Bian said. "According to the legend, the dragon-lord and fairy princess fell in love and had one hundred perfect sons. When the children grew up, the oldest son became the first emperor of our country."

Clay smiled. "That's a cool story," he said. Then he added, half-jokingly, "But if Vietnamese people are descended from a dragon, why don't they all look like dragons?"

"I used to ask my grandmother the same thing," Bian said. "She always said it was because we also have the blood of the fairy princess in our veins. On the outside we look like humans, but on the inside we have the heart and soul of a dragon."

The next exhibit featured Buddhist dancers in white and yellow robes. The dancers swirled to the beat of a drum to show the conflict between spirit and flesh. When they were finished watching the dance, Clay said, "I'm hungry."

"Again?" Bian asked.

"Yeah, I'd like to try some rice cakes," he said.

Bian was pleased someone she knew was actually willing to try one of her favorite Vietnamese foods.

"These are great," Clay said, taking a

bite of his third rice cake. "What did you say they're called?"

"Banh chung," Bian said, starting her second. "I'm glad you like them."

"You know, this has really been fun," Clay remarked. "The Vietnamese culture is such an interesting one. How do you say 'thank you' in Vietnamese, Bian?"

"Cam on nhieu," Bian said.

"Then *cam on nhieu*, Bian," Clay said. *"Cam on nhieu* for coming with me today."

They spent the rest of the afternoon looking at exhibits from other cultures. By the time they reached the Korean exhibit, Clay was hungry again.

"Let's get some egg rolls," Clay said. "I remember eating those when I lived in Korea. They called them *man-du.*"

"Man-du," Bian repeated. "Now you are teaching me," she laughed.

The afternoon went by too quickly. At 4:45 they headed for the parking lot. When they got in the car, Clay turned to Bian and said, "One more question. How do you say 'I like you'?"

Bian looked down. "You are embarrassing

me," she said.

"No, really, how do you say it?" Clay pressed.

"Well, 'I like you' is *toi qui ong lam*," Bian answered.

Clay took Bian's hand and looked into her eyes. *"Toi qui ong lam,"* he said.

Bian didn't know what to say. She obviously liked Clay too. But in Vietnam a girl would be considered forward if she told a boy on the first date that she liked him.

"Cam on nhieu," was all she could bring herself to say.

When Bian got home, she went straight to her room. She was excited and happy, ashamed and frightened, all at the same time. She had known happiness before. She had been happy when she and her family arrived safely in the United States. She had been happy when she received her first bicycle and even happier when she earned an A in English as a Second Language class her first year at school. But none of this happiness compared to what she felt now. She felt as if she would burst with this happiness, as if from here on out nothing in her life could possibly be difficult or disappointing. With this kind of happiness, Bian was certain that she'd never be lonely, never feel rejected, never feel inferior again.

But as fast as the happiness blossomed, it was weeded out by shame and fear. Lucy was her best friend. She had offered Bian friendship when no one else would, when the other kids looked at her black hair and almond-shaped eyes as if she were something to be frightened of. Lucy had always been there for her. They had been in Scouts together, taken dance lessons together, grown up together these last five years. And Bian had stolen Lucy's boyfriend. Even if Clay didn't like Lucy, Lucy liked Clay, and Bian had no right to come between Lucy and her efforts to win Clay over.

The worst part was there was no one she could share her conflicting feelings with. Lucy, of course, was out of the question. And Bian's parents would never accept her strong feelings for Clay— not to mention her betrayal of Lucy's friendship.

Suddenly Bian thought of Thien. Why hadn't she thought of him before? He would be an objective voice, someone who wouldn't judge her too harshly but would offer advice if she asked for it.

"See what this dating business leads to?" Thien said after Bian had explained what had happened. "Now you are falling in love with Clay. It gets worse by the minute!"

"Oh, Thien, what should I do?" Bian cried.

"Simple. Apologize to Lucy immediately and make up your mind never to see Clay again."

"I tried making up my mind not to see Clay before—it didn't work," Bian admitted.

"Then I have no more advice for you," Thien said.

Bian hung up the phone. Thien was right. The best solution was to beg forgiveness from Lucy and forget Clay. Then Lucy would be happy, Bian's parents would be happy—and Bian would be miserable. How could a solution be right that ended with her being so unhappy?

She made up her mind to do nothing for now. Maybe Lucy wouldn't be as angry as Bian feared. Maybe seeing Bian with Clay had made Lucy realize that her own relationship with Clay was not meant to be.

That night Bian went to sleep hopeful—hopeful that she hadn't lost her best friend and hopeful that she would see Clay tomorrow.

7 The next morning, Lucy was just closing her locker as Bian walked up.

"Lucy?" Bian said uncertainly.

Lucy turned and glared at Bian. "How could you?" she demanded. Without waiting for an answer, she turned and walked away.

Bian sighed. Whatever hope she had gone to sleep with last night deserted her now. Later at lunch, Bian got the cold shoulder from Trish and Bethany and ended up eating alone. The only bright spot in her day was when she saw Clay between fifth and sixth periods.

"You want to go for an ice cream after school?" Clay asked.

"Um, sure," Bian answered, but she knew they would have to make it quick. Normally her parents expected her home right after school unless she told them otherwise. She didn't want to be too late, or she would have to explain why.

After school, Bian rode her bike to Swan's. She was glad to see that Lucy wasn't there. She sat down in a booth and waited for Clay. Twenty minutes later, he arrived.

"Hi," he said, sitting down. "Sorry I'm late. I had to finish my lab report for chemistry."

"That's all right," Bian said. She glanced at her watch. She figured she had about twenty minutes before she had to leave if she wanted to avoid questions from her parents.

Clay ordered a huge banana split, and Bian ordered a small chocolate cone that she could eat in a hurry. They talked about the ethnic fair they had been to. Bian enjoyed reliving their first "date" and felt the happiness from the day before returning. Suddenly losing her other friends didn't seem to be too high a price to pay as long as she could be with Clay.

"How are you doing on your journalism project?" she asked.

"Great," Clay answered. "You gave me so much help at the ethnic fair that I should be able to finish it in a few days. I think it'll be one of my best projects." Then he changed the subject.

"My brother and I are having a beach party Saturday afternoon. We're going to roast hot dogs, do some surfing, and just generally hang out." He reached over and covered her hand with his. "I'd really like you to come. Think you can?"

"What time?" Bian asked. She knew that her parents would want to know.

"We'll probably start about 1:00 and go 'til 9:00 or 10:00," Clay answered.

"I don't know," said Bian. "I'll ask." Suddenly she remembered to recheck her watch. She had been there over an hour!

"I've got to go, Clay," Bian said, rising. "My parents will wonder where I am."

"Okay, but remember to check and see if you can go to the party with me," Clay said.

"I will. Bye!" Bian hurried outside and jumped on her bike. She pedaled home as fast as she could. As she walked in the door, her mother was setting the table for supper.

"I'm sorry," Bian said.

"Where have you been?" Mr. Tran asked. He was sitting at the desk in the corner of the kitchen writing a letter to a relative in Vietnam.

"Um, I stopped and got an ice cream,"

Bian answered.

"With Lucy?" her mother asked, handing Bian the plates.

Bian hesitated. "Yes, with Lucy," Bian said. She hated to lie to her parents, but she knew that if they found out she was with "an American boy," she may never get to see Clay again. Bian was not willing to risk that.

"Next time you are going to be late, call us," Mrs. Tran said. "You know how we worry."

"I will, Mother," Bian said.

At dinner, Bian decided to broach the subject of Clay's beach party. "Some friends are having a party at the beach Saturday afternoon. May I go?"

"What will you do there?" Mr. Tran asked.

"Oh, roast hot dogs and things. Some of the kids will go surfing, but of course, I would never do such a thing."

"Will Lucy be there?" Bian's mother asked.

"No, these are some different friends," Bian answered.

"Friends from school?"

"Some of them," Bian answered. At least Clay is, she told herself.

"What time is it over?" Mrs. Tran asked.

"About 9:00 or 10:00," Bian answered.

"Too long to be there," her father said flatly. "I will permit you to go, but you must be home by 7:00. But remember, no surfing!"

Bian was thrilled. Another day with Clay! She knew she should have told her parents the entire truth, that she was going with a boy who was special to her. But she was afraid her father would have said no. Bian made up her mind to tell her parents about Clay very soon. They were impressed with Clay when they met him. Maybe gradually, Bian could work Clay into their mealtime conversations. Once they got used to hearing his name, she could tell them how special he was to her. Then everything would be open and honest again.

At school the next day, Bian told Clay that she could go to the beach party.

"But could you pick me up at the library instead of at home?"

"Well, sure," Clay said. "But why?"

"Um, I have to go to the library anyway," Bian lied. She didn't want to tell Clay that her parents might not approve of their seeing each other again. "I've got a report due for English."

* * *

The week dragged by for Bian. For one thing, she was excited about Saturday, so every day seemed like an eternity. But for another, she felt so alone all week. Lucy, Bethany, and Trish continued to give her the cold shoulder. She had approached Lucy a couple of times, but Lucy had refused to talk to her. Now Bian had no one to gossip with or sit with at lunch, and no one to walk to class with. Time passes so slowly when one is lonely, she thought to herself.

Saturday Bian packed a bag for the beach and left the house. She told her parents she had some work to do at the library before the party and that her friends were picking her up there. She stuck a spiral notebook in the bag for effect. They accepted her explanation without question, making Bian feel a little guilty as she got on her bike. But as she pedaled toward the library, thoughts of seeing Clay again soon preoccupied her mind.

At the library, she locked her bike up to the bike rack and was waiting on the steps of the library as Clay pulled up.

"Hi!" Clay said as he got out to open her door.

What a gentleman, Bian thought. "Hi," she said.

"What a day, huh?" Clay asked. "Eighty degrees and pure sunshine. Man, California's great, don't you think?"

"Yes, I do," Bian said.

"What's the weather like in Vietnam?" Clay asked as they drove toward the coast.

"My family is from a small village on the southern coast," Bian explained. "Our climate is tropical. The monsoons bring us lots of rain, and the humidity is very high. You have less humidity here in California. I like that."

"I'd love to see Vietnam some day," Clay said. "Is it pretty?"

"Oh, yes, very pretty," Bian assured

him. "Everything is so green. The jungles are especially beautiful. They are filled with exotic flowers and birds you do not have in this country."

"Who knows? Maybe I'll become a foreign correspondent and get there someday." Clay had a wistful tone to his voice.

"That is a wonderful dream," Bian said. "I hope you do."

When they reached the coast, Clay took Bian's bag and then reached out for her hand. He led her down a rocky path to the beach. A group of kids were spreading out blankets and lawn chairs on the sand. One boy was starting a fire, and a pretty blonde girl was unpacking a picnic basket. Several surfboards lay on the beach nearby.

"Hey, Brad!" Clay called to the boy over the fire. "That's my brother," he said to Bian. Bian could see a slight family resemblance.

"Hey, Clay!" the boy yelled back. "Who's that with you?"

Several people looked their way, but Bian didn't recognize any of them. She was suddenly self-conscious.

"This is Bian Tran," Clay said. "She's my date."

"Hey, Bian," three or four people called. The others smiled or nodded her way. Bian relaxed. It made her feel good to hear Clay announce that she was his date. Bian smiled back at them.

"Isn't this great?" Clay said, pulling off his T-shirt.

"Clay! Let's go!" yelled one of the guys who was heading down the beach with a surfboard.

"Do you mind?" Clay asked Bian.

"Not at all," Bian said. "I'll watch." She spread her towel on the sand and sat down.

Clay grabbed a board and ran into the surf, hopping over the foamy tide. When the big wave roared in, Clay was positioned on his board, riding the crest, balanced perfectly and, Bian noticed, looking great. When he had caught a few waves, he came back in, vigorously toweling himself dry. Then he spread his towel out next to Bian's, grabbed a handful of potato chips, and laid back on the sand. "I love the water," he said, munching on a chip.

"Mmm, it's beautiful here," Bian said.

"Are you interested in learning how to surf?" Clay asked, turning over on his stomach. "I could teach you."

Bian remembered her father's warning. "I don't think so," she said. "For one thing, I would be too scared. It looks pretty risky to me."

"I was scared at first too," Clay admitted. "But once I got used to it, I was okay. Now I love it. I figure that's what life's all about—reaching out and grabbing experiences. Once you beat the fear, you're a winner, right?"

The rest of the afternoon passed quickly. Clay spent quite a bit of time surfing, but he made sure that in between he sat with Bian. They talked about their families, school, and the latest movies they'd seen.

About 5:00, Brad, the official "tender of the fire," announced that the coals were perfect for cooking hot dogs and marshmallows.

"Good!" Clay said. "I'm starving!"

"And what else is new?" Bian teased.

Clay laughed. "You're funny—shy and funny at the same time. I like that."

The smell of roasting hot dogs and marshmallows mingled with the salty air as everyone gathered to eat. Nearby a flock of seagulls hovered, waiting for someone to drop a piece of food. And farther down the beach, sandpipers raced to outrun the waves. This really is beautiful, Bian thought. No wonder Clay likes it so much.

When they were finished eating, Brad added some wood to the fire. Then he picked up a guitar and started playing an old Eric Clapton tune, "Wonderful Tonight."

"Brad's crazy about Clapton," Clay said. "He wants to play in a band someday."

Brad started singing the lyrics, and one by one people joined in. When they got to the line, *My darling, you were wonderful tonight*, Clay reached over, took Bian's hand, and looked straight into her eyes.

Bian was so happy. She felt as if a whole new world had opened up to her. A world that contained only Clay and her— not Lucy, not her other friends, not even her parents. It was a warm, accepting world, without pressure or criticism. Bian felt as if she could be happy in that world for a long time.

8 On the way home, Clay and Bian stopped to get Clay a malt. He, of course, was hungry again. Bian didn't want anything, so she waited in the car while Clay ran into the ice cream parlor.

From where she sat in the car, Bian had a clear view of the dead-end alley in back of Swan's. Suddenly she heard the roar of a motorcycle. Bian turned her head and looked up the alley. It was the same scene she had seen before. A white pickup truck blocked the alley. Buffalo was on his Harley, gunning the engine and yelling at the two boys. Only this time, Gavin and Tom were out of the truck, standing in front of the motorcycle.

"I told you to get out of my way," Buffalo yelled.

"And we told you last time you're a dead man, Grandpa!" Tom said.

"You have no idea what you're messin' with, you little sewer rats," Buffalo warned.

"That's where you're wrong," Gavin said. "We know exactly what we're messin' with. Just because you've been in Vietnam doesn't make you special. You're just an old man with a ponytail." As he spoke, he reached into his jacket and pulled out a knife with a long blade. "I think it's high time you had a haircut."

"I'm warning you for the last time," Buffalo said between clenched teeth.

Bian looked around frantically, but the street was deserted. Suddenly the two boys rushed at Buffalo from his left. Bian saw Buffalo swerve his handlebars sharply to the right and rev his motor. Suddenly Gavin was on the ground, clutching his leg. Tom stood frozen, seemingly in a state of shock. Buffalo headed down the alley, kicking up gravel and dirt behind him. As he roared past, Bian sank down into the seat, hiding her face from view.

Bian couldn't believe what she had just witnessed. She began to sob, quietly at first and then uncontrollably. A few minutes later, Clay was beside her. He gathered her into his arms until the sobbing subsided. "What happened, Bian?" he asked. He evidently had not heard anything from inside the ice cream parlor.

Bian heard sirens wailing in the distance. Tom must have gotten to a phone and called for help. Bian was so scared, she couldn't think. She just wanted to get as far away from there as possible.

"Take me away from here, Clay," she begged. "Please!"

"Okay, okay," Clay said soothingly. "I will." He started the car and pulled away from the curb.

Clay drove to a secluded spot near a park a few blocks away. He turned off the car and turned to Bian. "Now will you tell me what happened?" he asked, lifting her chin.

Bian took a deep breath. "Do you know who Buffalo Fraser is?" she asked.

"Sure," Clay answered. "He's that old guy who rides around on a Harley."

"That's right," Bian said. She had to take another deep breath before she could bring herself to say, "I just saw him run down Gavin Hicks with his motorcycle."

"You what?" Clay asked incredulously.

"I saw him hit Gavin Hicks, the basketball player from our school." She explained the whole incident to him, how Gavin and Tom had come at Buffalo and how he had tried to swerve around them but had accidentally hit Gavin.

Clay put his arms around her. "No wonder you were upset," he said. "Is that what those sirens were for?"

Bian nodded. "That's why I had you take me away from there," she said. "I knew Tom had gotten help. But now I realize I must go back and tell what happened."

"What will you say?" Clay asked.

"That Gavin and Tom threatened Buffalo and that he hit Gavin as he was trying to escape."

Clay was silent for a moment. "Are you sure you want to do that?" he asked.

"What do you mean?" Bian asked.

"Well, you had nothing to do with it," Clay began. "And you know what's going to happen when word gets out about Gavin. Everyone's banking on him to help win the state tournament. Everyone's going to want to string up Buffalo Fraser—and anyone who defends him. I'd hate to see you be the brunt of all that anger."

"But I must tell what happened," Bian insisted. "Buffalo Fraser was the victim here—not Gavin or Tom."

"Buffalo Fraser is a menace to society," Clay said. "He's also a bigot. Lucy's brother told me all about him."

"You know that he is Lucy's grand-father?" Bian asked, surprised.

"Yeah, and I also know he's a danger-ous character. Vietnam seems to have done a number on his mind."

"Still . . ." Bian began.

"And Gavin and Tom aren't much better," Clay added. "You know how they treat the kids at school who are different from them. Remember when Tom tried to spike your punch?"

"Yes, but . . ."

"Look, Bian, I'm not trying to tell you what to do," Clay said. "I'm just trying to point out both sides of the issue."

"But it's the right thing to do. In my

heart I know it," Bian said.

"That might be," Clay said, "but is it the *safe* thing to do? I'm just saying that maybe sometimes doing the safe thing is more important than doing the right thing. I don't want to see you get hurt."

"I am so confused," Bian said.

"Why don't you just go home and sleep on it?" Clay suggested. "Then in the morning if you still feel it's the right thing to do, you can go to the police station and make a statement. I'll even drive you there if you want me to."

Bian panicked at the word "home." "Oh, my gosh, what time is it?" she cried.

"7:45," Clay answered.

"Take me back to the library, please!" Bian said.

A few minutes later, Clay pulled up to the curb in front of the library. As she hurried to climb out of the car, he caught her by the shoulder. "Remember, Bian," he said. "I'm here for you no matter what you decide to do. *Toi qui ong lam.*"

This time Bian didn't hesitate. Her feelings for Clay were real, she told herself, and she wanted him to know it.

"Toi qui ong lam, Clay," she said. She grabbed her bag, sprinted to the bike rack, and rode home faster than she had ever ridden before.

"I am sorry, I am sorry," she was already saying as she came through the door. Her parents were in the living room waiting for her. Her father looked angry.

"You are almost an hour late," he said in Vietnamese. Even though he didn't ask for it, Bian knew he was demanding an explanation.

Bian hesitated. She wanted desperately to tell her parents what had happened tonight. But if she told them, they would know she went with Clay to the ice cream parlor. And even though she was feeling more confused and scared than she ever had in her whole life, her feelings for Clay prevailed above it all. Again, she found herself unwilling to risk not being able to see him again.

"I lost track of time," she said. "We were having such fun." She smiled in an effort to be more convincing.

Mr. Tran was unmoved. "This is the second time you have been late this week," he reminded her. "Next weekend you will stay home."

Bian swallowed hard. She knew it was no use arguing. "Yes, Father," she said obediently. She turned and went to her room.

Bian threw herself on her bed. How could she be so happy one moment and so miserable the next? she wondered. What if Clay wanted to do something with her next weekend? How could she explain to him that her parents had grounded her for coming in at 8:00 on a Saturday night?

Then she remembered the events of the evening and felt even more dejected. How was Gavin doing? she wondered. Where was Buffalo Fraser? Despite their bigotry, her heart went out to both of them. Oh, why had she agreed to go to the ice cream parlor with Clay? If she had insisted on going straight home, she wouldn't be going through this now.

But the most important question on

Bian's mind was what was she going to do? Clay was right. If she told the police what she knew, she might be the object of scorn or even violence. But if she didn't tell, an innocent man might be punished. Could she live with that?

She stayed in her room until 10:00 when she came out to brush her teeth. Her parents were in the living room watching the news.

"Bian, come here," her mother called. "They are talking about a boy from your school—and Lucy's grandfather!"

With a sinking feeling, Bian entered the living room and looked at the television. A reporter was standing at the scene, her face grim as she spoke. "I'm standing in the alley behind Swan's Ice Cream Parlor at 14th and Pierce. Gavin Hicks, a popular basketball player from Drake High School, was run down by a motorcycle here earlier this evening. According to Tom D'Angelo, Hicks' companion, the two boys were accosted by one Barry Fraser, who goes by the name of Buffalo."

The scene switched, and Bian realized

that she was seeing the front of Lucy's house on the screen. Police were leading Lucy's grandfather out of the house and into a squad car.

"Fraser was arrested at the home of his daughter—a Mrs. Lorraine Como—about an hour ago," the reporter went on. "According to sources, he's been charged with willful injury, which carries a mandatory prison sentence of a maximum of ten years."

Now the reporter was on the screen again. "Hicks' leg bone was shattered in the incident," she read from the notes in her hand. "He was taken to Central Hospital where he is undergoing surgery."

The scene switched back to the station's anchorman who turned to the sportscaster.

"That's certainly going to be a blow to Dragon fans, Heidi," the anchorman said.

"Yes, indeed," Heidi Shore answered. "As you know, Ron, the Drake Dragons are headed for the state tournament next week. The loss of Hicks as their center could put a real dent in their offense. He's consistently been one of their top scorers this season. Here's some footage from last week's win against Lincoln for the district championship."

Bian watched as Gavin was shown slam-dunking several baskets and making a three-pointer from well outside the circle.

"Oh, my," Mrs. Tran said. "This is terrible. Why would Mr. Fraser do such a thing? Do you know the boy, Bian?"

"Not really," Bian said, feeling sicker by the minute. Buffalo Fraser arrested! Mandatory prison sentence!

Bian could not watch the television any longer. "Good night," she told her parents.

"Bian, are you all right?" her mother asked. "You look like you don't feel well."

"I am fine, Mother," Bian said. "I'm just feeling bad for Gavin and for Lucy." She brushed her teeth and went to bed, feeling more exhausted than she had felt in a long time.

Bian slept poorly that night. In her dreams, she relived those terrible moments in the alley when she had seen

Gavin take the knife out of his jacket. Then she saw the boys laughing and heading straight for Buffalo. And over and over, she heard the rev of the motorcycle and saw Gavin drop to the ground, clutching his leg.

When Bian arrived at school on Monday, everyone was talking about what had happened. As she entered the building, she passed a knot of students standing by the vending machines. Tom D'Angelo was in the middle of the group telling his version of the story.

"We were hanging out in the alley," Tom was saying, "when this madman on a motorcycle comes rushing toward us, like he owns the place or something. We try to talk to him and tell him to, like, chill out. The next thing I know, he runs Gavin down. Then he blasts out of the alley doing about ninety."

"Man," one of the students said, "why do they let weirdos like that roam around? He should have been locked up a long time ago."

Bian winced at the total lie Tom had

told. Gavin and Tom had come at Buffalo, not the other way around. The boys had ambushed the older man, and Bian was the only one who knew that.

As Bian approached her locker, she saw Lucy heading toward the girls' restroom, tears streaming down her face. Poor Lucy, Bian thought. How humiliated she must be. Last week, Bian had been one of the few students who had known that Buffalo was Lucy's grandfather. Now everyone knew. How awful to have the whole school know that your grandfather seriously injured one of the star athletes!

Bian automatically headed for the restroom to offer comfort to her friend but then stopped. Even if Lucy didn't rebuff her, how could Bian discuss what had happened as if she knew no more about it than anyone else? And she couldn't tell Lucy what she had seen, or she'd have to tell the police as well.

But how could she *not* tell what she had seen? she asked herself. After all, Buffalo Fraser was innocent. And Lucy was her friend, even if they had hard feelings between them over Clay. She had to tell what she had seen. It was the right thing to do.

But just that fast, she remembered what Clay had said: "Maybe sometimes doing the safe thing is more important than doing the right thing."

Bian stood there a few minutes feeling as if she were being torn in two. Finally, she turned and walked away. The secret she held smoldered inside of her like a branding iron.

9

Bian avoided Clay that day. Once she saw him heading toward her, but she ducked into the girls' locker room. When she came out, he was gone.

She wasn't sure why she avoided him. Her feelings for him hadn't changed. But maybe it was because he was the only one who knew her secret, and she was afraid he would question her about what she had decided. She wasn't ready to discuss it with anyone.

Bian hurried home from school when classes ended. She headed straight for her bedroom with the excuse that she had a lot of homework. She had to be alone to think this thing through.

On the way to her room, she passed the shelf on which her mother kept the family pictures. The snapshot of Bian's grandmother caught her eye, and she stopped and picked it up.

Bian had always liked the picture. It was a good likeness of the small, spry woman with a gleam in her eye. She wore a straw field hat and a simple cotton blouse, and smiled out at the world with a missing front tooth.

Bian remembered Grandmother telling her stories when Bian was small. She would hold Bian in her lap, rock her back and forth, and weave magical tales about lucky turtles and wise old dragons. She had loved those times and had always felt safe and warm in her grandmother's arms.

Now as she held the snapshot, Bian thought back to the day it had been taken, the day the Tran family had left Vietnam. Bian's grandmother had insisted that Bian and her mother and father move to the United States. "There is nothing here for Bian," Grandmother had said. "You must go to the United States—plenty of opportunity for her there." She had even given them money for airfare from the meager savings she had managed to stash away before the war.

Bian's father had begged his mother to come with them to the United States, but she had refused. "I am too old," Grandmother had said. But Bian knew the real reason was because she could not bear to leave behind what she called her "work."

Vietnam was a poor country that had never recovered from the vicious war that nearly destroyed it twenty years earlier. Most of the fighting during the war had taken place in South Vietnam, where Bian's family had lived. The chemicals that were used to clear the jungles there scarred much of the area, permanently damaging the cropland and wildlife. The people who remained lived in extreme poverty, their homes destroyed, their lives shattered. Disease and starvation became a way of life for them.

Bian's grandmother had received some nurse's training as a young woman. After the war, she devoted her life to helping those around her. She cared for her own family, as well as for the people in her village who were sick or injured. After her children grew up, she traveled from village to village on foot, administering to those who needed her help. She even started an orphanage in the area for war orphans.

When Bian's father chided the old woman for working so hard, she would say, "What I do is right. That is all that matters." Many times as a child, Bian had received this advice from her grandmother. "Do what is right, my child. In the end, it is all that matters."

The day they left was a sad one. Bian's grandmother came to the airport to see them off. "Good-bye, Granddaughter," the old woman said as she held Bian in her arms for the last time. "Remember, your parents are going to the United States for your sake. Promise me you will not disappoint them."

"I won't, Grandmother," Bian promised, unable to control the tears that were streaming down her cheeks.

Bian's grandmother died a few months after the Tran family came to the United States. She had contracted malaria in one of the villages on her route. Bian remembered being filled with an almost overwhelming sadness for the brave little woman who had so often risked her life to help others. She knew she would never forget her grandmother. As Mr. Lamansky had said, some memories were forever.

Thinking about Mr. Lamansky made her remember her predicament—what should she do about Buffalo Fraser? Gazing at the picture, Bian found her answer. She knew that if she were to ask the old woman what to do, the old woman would simply say, "Do what is right."

Bian gently replaced the picture on the shelf. Then she turned and walked resolutely into the kitchen where her parents were. She took a deep breath and in a trembling voice said, "Mother, Father, I have something to tell you."

"What is it, Bian?" her mother asked, a look of concern on her face. "You look upset."

"Saturday night I saw the boy from my school get hit by Mr. Fraser's motorcycle."

Mrs. Tran let out a sharp cry of anguish. "You saw it? Oh, Bian!"

Mr. Tran frowned. "How could you have witnessed such a thing? Where were you when it happened?"

"That is why I did not tell you earlier," she said. "I was with Clay Monroe at the ice cream parlor."

"Bian!" her mother exclaimed. Mr. Tran raised his eyebrows.

Bian explained everything—from lying about going to the beach party to witnessing the incident. She even told them how Clay had tried to talk her into keeping quiet to avoid being subjected to the anger of others.

"But I could not do that," Bian said. "Lucy's grandfather was only trying to get away. It would not be right if he were sent to jail." She looked at her parents. "Can you ever forgive me?"

Her parents seemed to ignore her question. Finally her father said, "Come. You must go to the police station and tell them what you saw."

Bian hung her head in shame as she headed toward the car. At the police station, the three were taken into the office of Lieutenant Hayden, a detective in the homicide division. Lieutenant Hayden was a dark-skinned woman with close-cropped black hair. She smiled pleasantly at Bian and said, "Tell me exactly what you saw."

Bian began her story. "I was sitting in my friend's car waiting for him to come out of the ice cream parlor. The car was parked next to the alley behind Swan's. From where I was sitting, I could see into the alley."

Bian paused to take a deep breath. Even though Lieutenant Hayden was very nice, Bian was nervous. She had never been in a police station before.

"Go on, Bian," the detective said.

"A white pickup truck was blocking the alley like before. Only this time Gavin and Tom were out of the truck," she continued.

"Wait a minute," Lieutenant Hayden said. "Like before? You saw the boys in the alley at another time?"

"Yes, a couple of weeks ago. Gavin Hicks and Tom D'Angelo were in the truck. They were making fun of Lucy's—I mean Mr. Fraser. They wouldn't let him out of the alley."

"What happened?"

"It was amazing," Bian said, shaking her head. "Mr. Fraser rode his motorcycle off the loading dock in back of the ice cream store. He sailed over the pickup truck and got away."

Lieutenant Hayden smiled. "Somehow that doesn't surprise me, having met

Buffalo. Please go on, Bian."

"Again, Gavin and Tom would not let Mr. Fraser out of the alley. But this time, when Mr. Fraser yelled at them to get out of his way, Gavin pulled a knife out of his coat. He said he was going to give Mr. Fraser a haircut."

"What did the knife look like, Bian?" Lieutenant Hayden asked.

"It had a long blade—maybe twelve inches long."

The detective made a note of what Bian had said. "What happened next?" she asked.

"I'm not sure. It all happened so fast. I heard Mr. Fraser rev up his motor and turn his handlebars to get around the boys. The next thing I knew, Gavin was on the ground, and Mr. Fraser was riding away."

"What was Tom doing?" Lieutenant Hayden asked.

"He was just standing there, looking stunned," Bian said. "A few minutes later, I heard the ambulance coming. When my friend came out of the ice cream parlor, I asked him to drive me away from there—

I was so scared!"

"I'm sure you were," the detective said soothingly. "But I have one more important question to ask you, Bian. After the incident, did you see what happened to the knife?"

Bian shook her head. "No," she said. "When Mr. Fraser came out of the alley, I hid my head so he would not see me. I stayed that way until my friend came back." Then she asked, "So you will let Mr. Fraser go now?"

"We'll investigate what you told us, Bian," Lieutenant Hayden said. "The problem is, both Tom and Gavin deny having any kind of weapon, and we haven't been able to find one. So it's just been their word against Fraser's. Now that you've come in and made a statement, we'll definitely keep looking."

Lieutenant Hayden came around her desk and shook Bian's hand. "Thank you for coming in, Bian," she said. "It took a brave person to do what you did. You must be very proud of your daughter," she said, turning to Mr. and Mrs. Tran. Her parents simply nodded and thanked the lieutenant.

On the way home, the shame of what she had done behind her parents' backs returned to her. "You should not be proud of me," she said. "I have been deceitful, and I am ashamed."

"We are both proud and disappointed in you," Mr. Tran said. "You acted bravely and are to be admired for it. But in Vietnam it is a disgrace for a child to disobey her parents the way you did. You will stay home for four weekends instead of one."

Bian was shocked. A whole month? She thought about Clay. How could they go an entire month without being together? But again, she knew it was futile to argue with her father. She also knew that she probably deserved the punishment.

"Yes, Father," she said.

The next day at school, Lucy was waiting for Bian at her locker. Bian looked at her questioningly.

"Oh, Bian," Lucy burst out, "I'm so glad you came forward for my grandfather. His lawyer stopped by last night and told us what you did. Thank you so much."

"You are welcome," Bian said.

"But why did you do it?" asked Lucy. "I mean, after the trouble we've had over Clay and all. I figured you hated me now."

"Lucy, I never hated you," Bian said. "I was just hoping that eventually you'd understand."

"Actually, I've been wanting to talk to you about that for several days," Lucy said. "I finally realized that Clay never liked me. I was just dreaming. I guess I thought I could be Miss Popularity overnight. If he really likes you and you really like him, then the two of you should be together. Still friends?"

Bian smiled. "Still friends," she said.

Just then Bethany and Trish came by.

"You guys," Lucy said eagerly. "My grandfather's innocent. Gavin and Tom were threatening him with a knife. Bian saw it! He was just trying to get away."

"You're kidding," Bethany said. "Those guys had a knife? Well, I guess I'm not too surprised, now that I think about it."

No one had noticed that Mandy Owens, Gavin's girlfriend, was standing nearby. Now Mandy walked up to Bian and said,

"Is this your way of getting your friend back—by making up lies about what happened? I mean, I know you don't have many friends, but this is ridiculous."

Bian was confused. "No, I swear, I'm telling the truth," she insisted. "The boys had a knife."

"That's not true, and you know it," Mandy snapped. "It's bad enough poor Gavin is lying in the hospital with his whole future as a basketball player possibly ruined. He doesn't need people like you making up lies about him and taking that crazy man's side."

"My grandfather's not crazy," Lucy said. "He was in Vietnam. He saw horrible things—innocent civilians dying, villages burned to the ground, his best buddies blown up by land mines. You'd be affected by seeing those kinds of things too."

"Maybe," said Mandy. "But I wouldn't go around running down innocent kids!" She turned and walked away.

"Don't worry, Lucy," Bian said. "If your grandfather's innocent, they will let him go. You'll see."

"I hope so," Lucy said.

Rumors flew around the school that day. Mandy didn't waste any time spreading the story that Bian had gone to the police and lied about Gavin and Tom. Several times Bian saw students whispering about her. Others glared at her when she walked by. And in English she found a note that said "LIAR" lying on her desk when she walked in the room.

Bian didn't see Clay all day, and she was glad. She would not have wanted him to witness the treatment she was receiving. But as she biked home after school, Clay drove alongside her. "Pull over. I want to talk to you," he called through the window.

Bian stopped her bike at the curb, but when Clay approached she said, "I can't talk for long, Clay. I've got to get home."

"I'll only keep you a minute," Clay said. "So much for taking my advice about staying out of this, huh?"

"Like you said, Clay, life is about overcoming fear," Bian said. "I was afraid of telling the truth. But I overcame my fear and did what I thought was right."

"I knew you would," Clay said. "That's

the kind of person you are. I was just hoping you wouldn't. What did the police say?"

"That they'd keep looking for the weapon," Bian said.

"You're sure you saw a knife?" Clay asked.

"Positive," Bian said.

"Do you want to go look for it?" Clay asked.

"Look for it?" Bian had never thought of that.

"Yeah, I'll help you," Clay said.

Bian checked her watch. She knew she should go home. But if she could find the weapon, then everything would be solved. And they were only a few blocks away from the alley.

"Okay," she said. "But I've got to make it fast. My parents will be very angry if I'm not home in a few minutes."

Bian biked over to the alley behind the ice cream parlor while Clay drove along beside her.

"Let's ignore the obvious places since we don't have much time," Clay suggested. "The cops have probably searched them already. Look around. Is there some unlikely place where Tom could have stashed the knife?"

"How about in there?" Bian asked, pointing at a manhole cover in the concrete.

"Good thought," Clay said. He walked over to the manhole cover and pulled on the handle. It wouldn't budge. "Locked," he said. "Okay, where else?" His eyes scanned the area.

"On the roof?" Bian asked.

"No, look how steep the roof is. You can see there's nothing up there."

Bian studied the top of the building. A round metal stack about eighteen inches high and ten inches around stood up from the roof. "Maybe it's in the chimney," she suggested.

"I don't think Tom would have had time to climb up there and drop the knife in the chimney, Bian," Clay said. "Remember, he had already called the ambulance by the time we left."

"Not climb," Bian said. "You forget. Tom is an excellent shot. Maybe he was able to toss the knife up into that vent *before* he called for an ambulance."

"You think so?" Clay asked doubtfully. Then he shrugged. "It's worth a look, at least. Let's just hope it didn't fall all the way down in."

Clay climbed up on the loading dock and looked for a handhold to hoist himself onto the roof of the ice cream store. Seeing none, he looked at Bian and shrugged.

Bian glanced at her watch. "Hurry, Clay. I've got to go."

Clay glanced down the row of buildings adjacent to Swan's. "There we go," he said, nodding in the other direction. He jumped down from the dock and ran to the back of the men's clothing store. A garbage dumpster was parked next to a low spot in the roof. Clay climbed on top of the dumpster and pulled himself onto the building. From there he made his way slowly to the ice cream parlor, three buildings over.

"Be careful, Clay," Bian warned.

When Clay reached Swan's, he inched up the steep roof and looked down the chimney vent. "Bingo!" he yelled.

"Do you see it?" Bian said.

"It's wedged sideways in here," Clay called. "Good thing the blade was so long." He started to reach into the stack.

"No, Clay!" Bian called. "Leave it there for the police. We don't want to smudge the fingerprints."

"Good thinking," Clay said. A minute later he was back on the ground next to Bian. "You go on home. I'll get to a pay phone and call the police."

As Bian climbed onto her bike, she looked at Clay and smiled. "What?" he asked.

"I don't know," Bian said, shaking her head. "You're just really something to help me out like this."

Clay looked into Bian's eyes. "I told you—*toi qui ong lam*," he said. Gently he placed his hands on her shoulders, leaned down, and kissed her. Then he said, "Now go, before you get into trouble with your parents."

Bian pedaled home, smiling all the way. When she got home, her parents were working in the backyard so they didn't notice that she was a few minutes late.

Bian went straight to her room and threw herself onto her bed. She felt strangely elated as if something wonderful were about to happen. Was it because the knife had been found and Lucy's grandfather would probably be set free? she asked herself. Or was it because what Clay had done for her today proved he really did like her? Or was it simply because he had kissed her? Bian had no idea. She only knew that if she closed her eyes, she could still feel Clay's lips on hers. That was enough for now.

10 Lucy called that evening. "Bian, my grandfather's lawyer just called. He said Clay Monroe led the police to the knife. Now they might let my grandfather out of jail. Isn't that wonderful?"

"I'm so glad for your grandfather, Lucy," Bian said.

Bian watched the local news with her parents at 10:00. The anchorwoman gave an update on the incident.

"Police have located the weapon Gavin Hicks allegedly used to threaten Barry 'Buffalo' Fraser. Last Saturday night, Fraser admitted to hitting local basketball player Gavin Hicks with his motorcycle. Hicks, by the way, remains in the hospital in good condition after undergoing surgery on his leg. The incident occurred in the alley behind Swan's Ice Cream Parlor at 14th and Pierce. According to Fraser, Hicks and his friend, Tom D'Angelo, approached him with a knife, and he accidentally hit Hicks when he tried to get away. Until now no weapon had been found, but this afternoon, Clay

Monroe, a seventeen-year-old senior from Drake, led police to the knife. The weapon was wedged in the metal chimney vent on the roof of Swan's. Police think D'Angelo may have tossed the knife into the vent before help arrived. The knife was dusted for fingerprints and sent to the crime lab. Police should have the results of the fingerprint I.D. within twenty-four hours. Stay tuned to Channel 9 for further updates."

Just then Clay called. "Did you see the news, Bian?" he asked. "I'm a celebrity."

Bian smiled. "Yes, I know," she said.

"Isn't it great?" Clay asked. "Now everyone knows you were telling the truth. And Lucy's grandfather's off the hook."

"I'm so relieved, Clay," Bian said, thinking that maybe now the kids at school would stop looking at her with daggers in their eyes.

"Not to change the subject," Clay said, "but you remember the state tournament is Saturday at 11:00, don't you? Do you want to go? Keith Lee and Dana Manning are riding with me. I thought we might be able to go as a foursome."

Bian felt her heart sinking. She desperately wanted to go, but she knew she was grounded. Her mind raced as she tried to think of a way she could manage it without her parents finding out. Perhaps she could once again tell them she was going to the library. She had a big research paper coming up for history class, and she knew they would let her go, as long as they thought she was doing work for school. Bian was tempted. She wanted to be with Clay so much. But then she remembered how ashamed she was the last time her parents found out that she lied to them.

"I am sorry," Bian said. "I cannot go with you, Clay. I am grounded."

"Grounded?" Clay said, sounding disappointed. "But this is the state tournament. You don't want to miss it—Drake might not go again for years. Just ask, okay?"

Reluctantly, Bian said, "No, I cannot do that. You can tell me about the game next week. Good-bye, Clay."

Bian hung up the phone. When she turned around, her parents were watching her. They both seemed to know what she had just done.

Her father smiled. "You are getting more like your grandmother every day."

"Cam on nhieu," Bian said.

The rest of the week was a depressing one for Bian. The entire school was fired up about the state tournament. The halls were decorated, a special pep assembly was held, and all around her, students were making plans to attend. Lucy and Trish were going with Lucy's brother. They invited Bian, but of course she had to tell them no.

Friday after school Clay walked Bian out to her bicycle. "Are you sure you can't go?" he asked once more. "I really don't want to go without you." He reached out and took her hand. "Couldn't you just ask? Maybe they'd let you go."

As before, Bian's fingers tingled with electricity when Clay's hand touched hers. She was tempted to change her mind. It wasn't too late to tell her parents she was going to the library. But she knew she could not lie to her parents again.

"Clay, you don't understand," she began. "In Vietnam, punishments are not taken back. I disobeyed my parents and am being punished for it. I have to accept that—and so do you."

"All right, but I'll call you when I get back, okay?"

Bian smiled. "I'll be waiting," she said.

The next day Bian did her best to keep busy. Her father was not home, so Bian spent the day with her mother. Together they cleaned house in the morning. Then in the afternoon, her mother helped her work on a new blouse she was making. Bian had chosen a red silk fabric for the blouse. She was looking forward to wearing it to school on Monday.

About 4:00, Thien and his mother dropped by for an unexpected visit.

"Hey, Bian," Thien said. "Long time, no see."

"Hi, Thien," Bian said. She was glad to see him. After all she had been through with Clay, it was nice to be with a boy whose main interest was computers.

"Didn't go to the big game today, huh?" Thien asked.

"I'm grounded," Bian said. She explained to Thien all that had happened since the last time they had talked.

"I told you getting involved with Clay would get you into trouble," Thien teased.

Bian glanced at the clock and thought of Clay. He should be getting home from the tournament soon.

Just then the phone rang. Bian picked it up, expecting to hear Clay's voice on the other end. Instead it was Lucy, and she sounded upset. "Bian, have you heard what happened?"

"No, what?" Bian asked. Perhaps Lucy's grandfather had gotten himself into more trouble, she thought.

"It's Clay," Lucy said. "He was in an accident. He and the two kids riding with him were taken to the hospital."

Bian was stunned. Clay in the hospital? She had to go see him. She ran to find her mother, who was sitting in the kitchen with Mrs. Banh. Quickly she explained what had happened. "I have to go see him, Mother," she said. "Please allow me to go."

"But Bian, your father has the car," her mother said. "And it is too far for you to ride your bicycle."

Suddenly Bian heard Thien's voice behind her. "I will drive her," he volunteered.

Bian's mother hesitated. "All right," she finally said. "You can go. But be careful!"

When Bian and Thien got to the hospital, they were told that Clay was in room 345. Thien told Bian he would wait for her in the visitors' lounge.

"Thank you, Thien," Bian said. Then she hurried off to Clay's room.

As Bian approached the room, she saw a man and woman leaving. The woman smiled at her. "You must be Bian," she said. "I'm Clay's mother, and this is his father. He's told us a lot about you."

"It is nice to meet you," Bian said. "How is Clay?"

"The doctors tell us he's going to be

fine," Mr. Monroe said. "He's got a sore head from where he hit the side window, so they're going to keep him overnight for observation. But he should be home tomorrow."

Bian was relieved. "May I see him?" she asked.

"Of course," Clay's mother said. "I'm sure he wants to see you."

Bian hurried into the room. Clay was lying in the hospital bed with a bandage around his head. His eyes were closed, but he opened them when Bian said, "Clay?"

"Bian," he smiled.

"Are you all right?" Bian asked anxiously.

"I'm fine," Clay said. "Just a little banged up." He reached for her hand and covered it with his.

"Are you in pain?" Bian asked.

"No, a little groggy is all. The doctors gave me a painkiller."

"What happened?"

"I don't know," Clay began. "We were on the way home from the game. I started to turn onto the highway, when all of a sud-den—bam!—this car came out of nowhere, I swear."

"How are Keith and Dana?" Bian asked.

"Keith is fine. He was in the seat in back of me. They've already released him. But my parents told me that Dana Manning has a broken leg and a concussion. She was sitting next to Keith on the passenger's side.

"Poor Dana," Bian said.

"You should see my car," Clay smiled weakly. "The passenger door took most of the impact. It's a mess."

Suddenly Bian's heart felt as if it had stopped. If she had gone with Clay, she would have been sitting on the passenger side. Nausea rose within her. What might have happened to her? Would she be in the hospital right now with a broken leg and a concussion like Dana—or worse? Then Bian thought of her parents. They would have been so shocked to receive a phone call from the hospital when they thought she was at the library. How horrible it would have been for them!

"Don't you want to hear about the game, Bian?" Clay asked sleepily. "We lost, but then I guess everyone figured we would."

Bian was deep in thought and didn't answer. She had never even considered that something like this might have happened today. Clay was a good driver, but even good drivers have accidents. How could she have risked doing something like this to her parents? Not only would they have been devastated if she had been injured, but they would have been so disappointed in her.

Bian remembered her grandmother's words: "Your parents are going to the United States for your sake. Promise me you will not disappoint them."

Bian knew now that her parents were right and that Thien was right. She was too young to become so involved with a boy, even a wonderful boy like Clay. She had a future ahead of her. Getting mixed up with Clay would only jeopardize that future, no matter how much she wanted to believe otherwise. Look at what it had caused her to do already—lie to her parents and practically lose her best friend. She knew now that those kinds of complications would only keep her from focusing on what was important. She owed it to her parents to become all she could—and she owed it to her grandmother.

Bian glanced at Clay. He was sleeping peacefully. She couldn't help noticing how handsome he was, even with a bandage around his head. Having Clay for a boyfriend had been exciting and wonderful. But for now she knew she wasn't ready to pay the price such a relationship might demand of her.

Gently she slid her hand out from under his. As she rose to go, she bent over and kissed his cheek.

"Good-bye, Clay," she whispered in his ear. "*Toi qui ong lam.*"

A few minutes later, she was back in her driveway with Thien.

"Thank you, Thien," Bian said. "You are a good—and wise—friend."

Thien smiled. "Say, I've got a new software program on my computer. It's supposed to help you choose a college, and then it provides you with a list of all the scholarships available. You want to come over tomorrow and check it out?"

"Yes, I'd like that," Bian said. "It's probably about time I started looking into colleges. I'll be over after church."

"Great," said Thien. "See you then."

As Thien pulled away, Bian noticed the sound of a motorcycle approaching. Looking down the street, she recognized Lucy's grandfather coming toward her on his Harley. He pulled up to the curb, got off his bike, and crossed the yard to where she stood. Bian waited in silence, unsure of what this man who had always frightened her wanted.

"Are you Bian?" Buffalo asked. Bian nodded. "I stopped over at Clay Monroe's house the other day to thank him for locating the knife. He told me you had more to do with it than he did."

Buffalo paused and cleared his throat as if this were not easy for him. "And my lawyer tells me that it was you who came forward as a witness to what happened."

Again he paused and gazed up and

down the street. Finally he turned and looked Bian in the eyes. "I just wanted to thank you for what you did. I'm sure you took some flack from your classmates about this."

Bian breathed a sigh of relief. "You're welcome, Mr. Fraser," she said.

"And I also wanted to tell you that you're welcome at my house anytime," Buffalo went on. "My granddaughter Lucy speaks very highly of you, and I'm finally realizing that she's right."

"I would be honored to come to your house," Bian said, smiling.

"Oh, one more thing," Buffalo said, reaching into his pocket. "I bought this when I was stationed in 'Nam. I think it's about time I gave it to somebody." He handed Bian a small white box. Bian opened the box and saw a gold chain. A pendant in the shape of a peace symbol caught the sun as she lifted the necklace from the box.

"This is beautiful," Bian said, putting it on. "Thank you, Mr. Fraser."

"No, *cam on nhieu*, Bian," Buffalo said,

smiling. "I learned that in Vietnam. Pretty good after all these years, huh?"

"Yes, very good," Bian laughed.

Still smiling, Buffalo got on his motor-cycle. Then he turned to Bian and held up two fingers in the shape of a V. "Peace," he called, as he rode away.

Bian made the same sign. "Peace to you, Buffalo Fraser," she said and turned to walk into her house.

Novels by Anne Schraff

PASSAGES

An Alien Spring
Bridge to the Moon
    (Sequel to *Maitland's Kid*)
The Darkest Secret
Don't Blame the Children
The Ghost Boy
The Haunting of Hawthorne
Maitland's Kid
Please Don't Ask Me to Love You
The Power of the Rose
    (Sequel to *The Haunting of Hawthorne*)
The Shadow Man
The Shining Mark
    (Sequel to *When a Hero Dies*)
To Slay the Dragon
    (Sequel to *Don't Blame the Children*)
A Song to Sing
Sparrow's Treasure
Summer of Shame
    (Sequel to *An Alien Spring*)
The Vandal
When a Hero Dies

PASSAGES 2000

Just Another Name for Lonely
    (Sequel to *Please Don't Ask Me to Love You*)
Memories Are Forever
The Hyena Laughs at Night
Gingerbread Heart
The Boy from Planet Nowhere